# The Forever Horse

# The Forever Horse

## Stacy Gregg

HarperCollins *Children's Books*

First published in Great Britain by HarperCollins *Children's Books* in 2020
HarperCollins *Children's Books* is a division of HarperCollins*Publishers* Ltd,
HarperCollins Publishers
1 London Bridge Street
London SE1 9GF

The HarperCollins website address is
www.harpercollins.co.uk

1

ISBN 978–0–00–833235–8

Stacy Gregg asserts the moral right to be identified as the
author of the work respectively.

A CIP catalogue record for this title is available from the British Library.

Typeset in Baskerville MT by Palimpsest Book Production Ltd, Falkirk, Stirlingshire
Printed and bound in England by CPI Group (UK) Ltd, Croydon CR0 4YY

For Maalika

## CHAPTER 1

# *Going Once, Going Twice . . .*

The crowd gathered in the golden chamber of the famous Paris auction house had come tonight with their wallets bulging. Elegant ladies in sparkling evening gowns sat on high-backed gilt salon chairs, clutching bidding paddles in their manicured hands, while their well-dressed husbands sat beside them looking nervous at the amount of money they were about to spend. Already tonight a small fortune had gone under the hammer. The annual auction of works by the graduates of the Parisian School des Beaux-Arts always attracted the clever art collectors who knew that one day the paintings they picked up in this room for relative peanuts could snowball in value and be resold for millions.

Throughout the evening the bidding had been steady

but unremarkable. Now, though, there was an electric tension in the room as two men dressed in white coats and gloves carried the next painting to the front and placed it gingerly on the easel beside the auctioneer.

At the very back of the auction chamber, Maisie rose on tiptoes to get a better view. Crammed in, where it was standing room only, she was terrified she would do something dumb, like raising her hand to scratch her nose and bidding by mistake. There was no way she could afford to buy this painting! Which was ironic, really, since Maisie was the artist who had painted it.

"Lot number sixty-seven!" the auctioneer, Monsieur Falaise, announced to his audience. "This substantial work, in oil on canvas, is entitled, *Claude*."

Monsieur Falaise, a thin man with a pointy chin, scanned the faces of the wealthy art patrons and felt certain that he knew which bidders would raise their paddles for this one. Over the years, he had developed an instinct for such things. So far tonight, he had watched as the bidders fought over various works of modern art – abstract and bold. This new painting, *Claude*, was quite the opposite of all that had gone before. The portrait of the black horse was in the mode of the classical realist masters. It was so detailed, and so lifelike. To think that it had been painted by a thirteen-year-old girl! Monsieur Falaise shook his head in disbelief. The work was so mature, and it was not just that it was magnificent in its technicalities. No, it was the heart that it possessed. The painting was imbued with such a depth of emotion it was impossible to gaze upon it without being reduced to tears. Monsieur Falaise wasn't ashamed to say that his own eyes had welled up a little when he saw it for the first time. And even now, in the thrust and clamour of the auction room as the bidders prepared themselves for the fierce battle ahead, he could see the patrons dabbing their eyes to quell their tears as a profound solemnity filled the room. For Claude, the subject of this remarkable work of art, was more than just a horse. For the people of Paris he embodied so much of what made the city great; looking upon him made hearts break. And art that makes a heart break is always worth a fortune.

"Who will open the bidding at five thousand euros?"

At the back of the room Maisie let out a squeak. Five thousand euros! It was a staggering figure! The other works the crowd had bid on so far that night had been much cheaper. Most of them ultimately sold for less than two thousand euros. To launch the bidding straight off at such a high figure was surely madness? But Monsieur Falaise knew two things: he knew his audience, and he knew precisely what this painting, at centre stage right now, meant to the people of Paris. And he was right. Within a split second of the bid being announced there was a paddle held aloft in the front row in reply.

"I have five thousand bid!" Monsieur Falaise snapped into action. "*Alors!* We are underway! Who will give me six thousand?"

Straight away, another paddle went up.

"I have six, six. Who will give me seven? Yes! Seven . . ."

At the back of the room, Maisie watched silently as the price of the painting – *her painting* – continued to climb. Soon, the price was at ten thousand euros. Then it climbed higher still! Leaping up by a thousand euros at a time, again and again, until the bid rapidly reached twenty thousand. Even then, the paddle-holders didn't slow, and soon twenty became thirty and thirty became forty!

There was a moment, at forty-five thousand, when a woman in the front row wearing a Chanel suit and jet-black sunglasses, decided to trump all the other bidders and proclaimed in an icy tone that she was raising the bid to fifty-one thousand, and a mutual sigh of defeat swept the room. Then, a grey-haired gentleman in a cravat came straight back at her and proclaimed "Fifty-three!" and the bidding was off again!

All the while, as the price climbed ever higher, Maisie felt more and more anxious. In this room, with Claude's black eyes staring at her, she was suddenly gripped with claustrophobia and remorse. How ridiculous to come here now when the real Claude was in such pain and the clock was ticking! What had she been thinking?

Maisie turned to leave, but the crowd were pressed together like sardines.

"I'm sorry! I have to go!" She began to try and push her way out, but the occupants of the auction room were so intently focused on the drama that was unfolding before them they refused to budge. Maisie tried again, in French this time. "*Je suis desolé! Pardon, pardon . . .*"

Her pleading had no effect. Maisie could feel the room closing in on her, her heart racing in panic.

"Please! I have to go!"

And then, as if by a miracle, the crowd parted, and there was Nicole Bonifait, Maisie's patron, so-to-speak, right in front of her, clearing the people out of the way, grasping Maisie's wrist to guide her through.

"It's OK, Chou-chou," Nicole said. "Come with me now. I have you!" and Maisie felt Nicole's arms around her, ushering her through the crush, until a moment later they were out of the room into the foyer and then through the front doors, stumbling down the marble stairs on to the wide Parisian street below. Maisie was taking deep breaths, her hands on her knees as Nicole barked at one of the waiters at a pavement café nearby to bring them one of his chairs. *Tout de suite!!*

The waiter hastily obliged, and Nicole sat Maisie down in the middle of the street and told the waiter to bring them water.

"Here, drink this." Nicole gave a fluted glass full of fizzy water to Maisie, who gratefully slugged it back in a single gulp. Her head was spinning.

"I'm fine," Maisie insisted. "Nicole, I need to go –"

"*Oui, oui, Petit Chou-chou Anglaise*," Nicole soothed, "but take a moment first to catch your breath."

*Petit Chou-chou Anglaise.* Nicole's nickname for Maisie. It meant Little English Cabbage. When Nicole had first told Maisie this, she thought it perhaps was supposed to be an insult, but Nicole assured her it was quite affectionate! Nicole Bonifait was half-British herself, as she'd pointed out to Maisie when they'd first met. And in a way, it was Nicole's English ancestry that had created the art scholarship that had changed everything and set Maisie off on this whole unbelievable adventure. Six months ago Maisie had been an ordinary schoolkid, living on a council estate in Brixton, South London. Now, here she was, sitting outside Lucie's, the most prestigious auction house in the whole of Paris, while the rich and the fabulous of the city tried to outbid each other over her art.

"Do you feel well enough to go back inside now?" Nicole asked her. "This is your moment of glory. Your work is going to fetch a record price, I think."

Maisie shook her head. "I'm not going back in. I don't care about the painting. I want to go back to Claude."

Nicole gave her hand a squeeze. "I understand completely," she said. "Who cares about a room full of bourgeoisie? Tonight, of all nights, you should be with him, no?"

"Yes," Maisie replied. "I'm not being ungrateful Nicole . . . I know how much this means to you . . ."

"Don't be silly, Chou-chou!" Nicole hugged Maisie

tight. "Go to him now! We have done what we can, but if these are truly to be his final hours you should be at his side."

Maisie found that her legs were surprisingly jelly-like when she rose from her chair, but she felt a steely determination that drove her on, made her put one foot in front of the other as she turned away from the auction house, heading down the boulevard Henri IV. Lucie's was walking distance from the stables of the Célestins, home to the mounted French police known as the Republican Guard. But as Maisie regained her strength that walk soon became a run. And it was as she was running that the tears began to come. She sniffled and choked as she wiped them away and kept running onwards through the crossroads. Car horns honked as she ignored the lights, cyclists yelled at her as she sped in front of their bikes. Then, at last, lungs aching, she reached the front gates of the Couvent des Célestins.

It was amazing to think that nearly two hundred horses lived right here in these opulent stables in the heart of Paris. These were city horses, accustomed to the hum and buzz of urban life, cared for by their riders, the noble gendarmes, the policemen of the Republican Guard.

Maisie was lucky. Alexandre, of all people, was on gate duty tonight – thank God! He had his feet up and was reading the paper and he got a shock when she knocked on the sentry box window to be let inside.

"Maisie?" He dropped the paper immediately. "I thought you were at the auction?"

Maisie's heart was still pounding from the run. "Alexandre, please? May I come in?"

Alexandre frowned. "You shouldn't be here, Maisie, not now . . . They will be coming for him soon."

Alexandre tried to resist but he could see the quiver of Maisie's bottom lip and the tear stains on her cheeks. He gave a sigh and reached beneath the desk of the sentry box, pressed the button, and the automatic doors swung open.

"If the guards come, you make yourself invisible, yes?" Alexandre looked hard at her, making his point clear. "You are not here."

"I am not here," Maisie agreed. "I am a shadow."

"That's my girl," Alexandre said. And then, with a wave of his hand, "Hurry now! A shadow moves quickly! Go to him!"

Maisie slipped briskly through the gates and across the courtyard, dashing between the clipped hedges and fountains to reach the stable block, sticking close to the walls where the security lights did not reach. She tiptoed across the cobblestones, creaked through the doors until, at last, she had made her way to Claude's stall.

"Claude?" Maisie spoke his name as she pulled the bolt and opened the door. Part of her was afraid at that moment that they would have sneaked in and come for him and he'd already be gone. But no. He was there. He nickered softly at the sight of her, and she met his dark, soulful eyes. The very same eyes she had recreated in the painting being auctioned right now at Lucie's.

Oh, but in real life he was so much more handsome! Of all the many beautiful and noble-blooded stallions who lived here in the stables of the Célestins, he was the most breathtaking. Jet-black with four white socks on his legs and a star on his forehead. A classic Selle Français, he had always turned heads when he was ridden on parade. That first day that Maisie had seen him, he had stood out above all the rest and she knew he was special – as indeed he had proved to be.

"Hello, my brave boy." Maisie spoke softly, and the stallion raised up his elegant crest to nicker to her. Then, exhaustion and pain overcame him and he let his mighty head fall between his forelegs like a dying swan in a ballet.

"Claude," Maisie knelt beside him and, using all her strength, she helped to lift his head, cradling him in her arms.

"I know you're in such pain, Claude," she whispered as she stroked his forelock, "but you won't need to be brave for much longer. I promise you, when they come for you, no matter how much it breaks my heart, I will stick by you. I'll be with you at the end. I promise, I promise . . ."

When Maisie had first come to Paris, she had marvelled at the beauty of this city. Her favourite time was the early morning when the sunrise washed the dove-grey rooftops an iridescent pink and the River Seine seemed to be made of molten gold. As an artist, she loved the dawn and its transformative, divine light. But tonight, as she held Claude tight in her arms, she dreaded the sunrise with all her heart. For when the night had ended, and the guards of the Célestins returned, Claude would be taken from her. And the light would be gone from Paris forever.

CHAPTER 2

# *The Thirteen-Million-Dollar Horse*

**One year earlier . . .**

The first horse I ever loved cost thirteen million dollars. And he wasn't even real. His name was Whistlejacket and he was a portrait hanging on the wall at the National Gallery in Trafalgar Square. OK, so it was the painting and not the actual horse that was worth all that money, but even so.

My dad had taken me to the gallery to look at Whistlejacket one rainy Sunday afternoon. I was five at the time – too young, really, to take to a gallery, but Dad says that's how he knew I was different from other kids, because instead of being bored I was in my element amongst all those famous paintings. I took in Van Gogh's brilliant yellow sunflowers, Claude Monet's soft and misty irises and Botticelli's languid reclining beauties, Venus and Mars – and I explained to Dad, my little-kid voice brimming with authority, exactly what techniques I envisaged the painters must have used, and what I liked about the composition and the colours. Dad says I was always certain about what I loved and hated about art, right from the start. I didn't get the abstract stuff, or the surrealists. I liked art that really looked like things – landscapes and animals and portraits.

There were some amazing paintings in the gallery that day, but when I saw Whistlejacket, they all disappeared, and he was everything to me.

He was a beautiful horse – deep chestnut with a flaxen mane and a thick honey-blond tail that flowed almost to the ground. There was one perfect white sock on his near hind leg and his haunches were muscled, but his limbs were delicate and his neck set perfectly into his elegant shoulders. As he reared up on his hind legs, he turned to look at me. His dark liquid-brown eye had such a soulful expression that it seemed impossible that he wasn't a real horse. To think that an artist had created all of this with his hands!

"I want to take him home," I told Dad, laughing.

"We can't," my dad said. "He belongs here, and besides – that painting's worth thirteen million pounds."

I was heartbroken until we went to the gift shop and Dad bought me a box of paints and a postcard of the painting.

"You can make your own horse now," he said.

That afternoon, I tried to paint my own Whistlejacket. I struggled hard to get the proportions right – to recreate his broad neck and the dip of his back and the curve of his rump. The legs were tricky! Especially his hooves. I found my new paints were a blunt instrument, too drippy and squishy, and so I swapped to a plain HB pencil. Using the pencil wasn't as colourful or fun, but I wasn't interested in painting like a little kid. I wanted to make my horse perfect, and with a pencil I could refine my picture, reworking the lines, rubbing out the bad patches and redoing them until I was satisfied.

I did lots of drawings of Whistlejacket, and each time I was finished I would show them to Dad and he'd put them on the fridge. At first they were pretty clumsy, but I got better fast. I mean, I was only five and most five-year-olds do drawings that just look like scribbles – but pretty soon I could do ones that really looked like a horse. I remember I did one that was really good, and it almost looked like him. My dad looked at it for a long time in admiration and then he said. "Maisie, you're a prodigy."

"What's a prodigy?" I asked.

"Someone who is very, very good at something at a very young age. Like Mozart."

"Did he draw horses then?"

"No. He played the piano."

"What's the point of being good at that?"

"Different people are good at different stuff," Dad said.

I decided at that moment that I would only ever be good at drawing horses.

The next weekend, we caught the bus to Hyde Park. Dad had bought me a new sketch pad with thick, white textured pages, and he'd made us lunch to take with us.

"There are horses here," Dad explained. "They keep them in stables not far away, and they're allowed to ride them through the park."

We sat on the grass beneath the trees that lined Rotten Row and waited, and within minutes we saw our first real-life horses! A pair of black-and-white cobs with fluffy feathered legs, Roman noses and broad backsides. I did a sketch of them as best I could as they went past, and then at home that night I painted over my original drawing to get the light and the colours right.

"Do you really think I'm a podgy?" I asked Dad. He was confused. Then he got what I meant.

"Not a podgy," he said. "Prodigy. It means you are a young genius. You have a gift."

So . . . yeah, I'm a prodigy. Or at least I was. If you look it up in wikipedia a prodigy has to be under ten! And I'm twelve now, almost thirteen, so I'm way over the hill – that is modern life for you. Anyway the prodigy thing is not all it's cracked up to be. You'd think that being an art genius would be a good thing. I mean, I'm pretty sure everyone loved Mozart when he was a kid. But it's totally not working out like that for me. For a start, Mrs Mason, my teacher at Brixton Heights Academy, is a total cow and thinks drawing in class is, like, a crime or something. As far as she is concerned, it would be better to be Adolf Hitler than to draw horses. At least that was the impression she gave at the parent-teacher conferences.

"She's wasting everyone's time and disrupting my class," Mrs Mason said.

"Because drawing horses isn't part of your art curriculum?" my dad asked.

"Mr Thompson," Mrs Mason said icily. "Maisie doesn't restrict her drawing to during art class. She is drawing horses all – the – time."

Mrs Mason reached below her desk.

"Maisie's maths book," she said as she held it up and flicked through the pages. There were no sums, no formulas on the cross-hatched pages. Just horses. Lots and lots of horses.

"I could show you her English book, which is exactly the same." Mrs Mason continued her character assassination. "She draws in science; even during religious studies! She is the most impossible, unteachable child I have ever encountered in all my years as an educator . . ."

Mrs Mason was so worked up that when the bell went off to signal it was time for the next parent, she ignored it! James McCavity, who was sitting with his mum in the row of chairs behind us, waiting for his turn, gave me a sympathetic smile as I sat there dumbly while she ranted. When the bell rang a second time and she was still going, teachers from the other classes who were in the school hall began to stop talking and

17

look over at Mrs Mason, who had got quite red in the face. And then, at last, when she had run all the way to the end of her tether, my dad spoke up.

"Did you ever look at her drawings, Mrs Mason?"

"I'm sorry?" Mrs Mason was confused. "What does that have to do with it? I'm talking about Maisie's bad manners in class."

My dad shook his head and sighed. "Are you aware that Maisie's mum died when she was a newborn?"

Mrs Mason looked taken aback at this. "I'm sorry," she stammered. "I wasn't . . . I didn't know."

"No. Of course not," Dad said. "So you didn't know that I'm a solo dad. I raise Maisie on my own and my time is tight. I work a sixty-hour week and I've had to make excuses to get off work early today. I came here expecting we were going to discuss what your school was doing to encourage and extend my gifted child."

"Mr Thompson!" Mrs Mason bristled back. "Even Picasso had to go to school you know."

Dad laughed and said, "You know what, Mrs Mason? You're dead wrong, but that's the one interesting point you've made today."

Afterwards, as we walked home, Dad told me about Pablo Picasso, one of the most famous artists in the world, and how Picasso was accepted into a fancy art school when he was just thirteen.

"I bet Mrs Mason wouldn't tell off Picasso," Dad grumbled.

"I think she probably would," I replied.

In a weird way, though, we had Mrs Mason to thank for what was to come. If it hadn't been for her, Dad would never have got the idea into his head that I could be like Picasso too. He was hatching a plan right there as we walked home, but he didn't talk about it with me yet. He just told me that Mrs Mason was a silly old sausage, and we got fish and chips and Dad told me to at least try and look like I was paying attention in class in future to keep Mrs Mason from calling him again.

He spent the rest of the night on the computer, and at one point I remember he came into the living room and began to sort through a stack of my drawings on the coffee table.

"Where's that one you did the other weekend?" he asked me. "Those two black-and-white horses trotting in the park with the big oak trees overhead? It's not on the fridge any more."

I always put my best works on the fridge and then

19

after a week or so I put them away in a drawer in my room. That was where I found the black-and-white horses.

Dad looked at the drawing and smiled. "This will do the trick," he said. I didn't know what he meant by that at the time, and I didn't think to ask.

For the rest of term there was a truce between me and Mrs Mason. It wasn't as if she started liking me or anything. That would have been too much to hope for. But she didn't keep looking over my shoulder to see what I was doing either. I think she couldn't be bothered facing down my dad again.

It was almost the end of term when Dad came home one evening and called me into the living room. There was something about the tone of his voice that had me really worried.

"Am I in trouble?" I asked when I saw him standing there with that serious look on his face.

Dad didn't say anything. He held out his hand and I saw the envelope. It was made of thick creamy paper embossed with a silver seal that had words in French on it.

"Is it for me? You've opened it already," I pointed out to him. The envelope was torn.

Then I saw he was shaking. There were tears in his eyes.

"Dad, is everything OK?" I was worried now. "What's going on?"

"You're in," he said.

"In what?"

"The School of Arts in Paris," Dad said. "A school term on a full, all-expenses-paid scholarship."

"But I didn't apply to art school," I said.

And then I remembered that day after the parent-teacher conference, when he'd searched out that drawing I did of the two black-and-white cobs.

"You didn't tell me you were going to apply to any art school," I said.

"I didn't want to get your hopes up," Dad said. "It's a scholarship for an English pupil to study there. They get over a thousand applicants – and only one kid gets picked."

"And they picked me?"

"They picked you," Dad confirmed.

"So, Maisie." He smiled at me. "What do you say? Do you want to go to Paris?"

CHAPTER 3

## *The Chance of a Lifetime*

We went out to a French restaurant to celebrate. It seemed appropriate, considering.

"The Parisian School of the Beaux-Arts is the most famous art school in the world," Dad said as the waiter handed us menus. I looked at the prices – eight pounds for a green salad!

"Did you win the lottery?" I asked.

"We deserve a special treat this once," Dad replied.

"But this Paris school," I pressed home the question. "What about that? Is it expensive?"

"Very expensive," Dad said. "But your fees and expenses for the term are paid for. That's what a scholarship means."

"So you don't have to pay anything?" I went back to the menu. "What are *l'escargots*?"

"Snails," Dad said. "Dare you to order them!"

I wasn't falling for that. I got burger and chips – in French it was called *steak haché* and *frites*. I could read the menu a little. I had taken French this year for the first time at school, and Dad always joked that the only words I seemed to retain in my brain were about food.

I squirted tomato sauce all over the *frites* as Dad explained to me about the scholarship.

"How will it work, though?" I asked. "If we have to go and live in Paris? How will you do your job?"

We were on the puddings by now. Dad had ordered the chocolate mousse. He gave it a prod with his spoon, but he didn't eat. He didn't speak for a bit either, and then he said. "It would just be you, Maisie. I need to stay and work – they won't hold my job for that long. You'd have to go alone."

I had just shoved a forkful of meringue in my mouth so I had to chew before I could reply.

"I can't go and live in Paris on my own. I'm thirteen!"

"I know," Dad said. "I'm not sure the scholarship people realised you were so young either. I think I forgot to fill in the bit with your age because in their reply they asked me what university you were currently attending!"

"Do you think they'll withdraw the offer when they find out?"

"I don't know," Dad admitted.

I felt my heart sink. "So I'm not going to Paris?"

Dad ruffled my hair.

"Don't fret yet, Mais," he said. "I'm going to talk to them. Perhaps there's a way we can make it work."

***

Let me tell you something about my dad. He is not a man who admits defeat. Yes, after he spoke to the Paris school, he said it had come as "a bit of a shock" to them when they found out I was only thirteen. Apparently they wanted to cancel my scholarship on the spot. Except for one woman who stood up for us. Her name was Nicole Bonifait – she was the great-great-great-granddaughter of Rose Bonifait, the artist who started the whole scholarship in the first place. Nicole Bonifait told them that she would take responsibility for me, acting as my guardian while I was in

Paris for the term. Then Dad spoke to my school in Brixton and they agreed to let me go on exchange (sucks to Mrs Mason!) and it was done!

One month later, I stood with my bags at Charles de Gaulle airport, being pushed this way and that as people hustled by me, surging through the arrivals terminal. I was in Paris! All. By. Myself.

And for a brief moment, standing there in the terminal, I felt entirely and utterly alone and completely terrified. And then, it was as if the crowds parted in front of me by magic and through the throng came Nicole Bonifait. Her flame-red hair was loose and bouncing on her shoulders as she hurried towards me.

"Welcome to Paris, Maisie," she said warmly as she grabbed my bags from the trolley. "Your life as an artist begins here and now."

***

We drove into the city round the Arc de Triomphe, and through the tinted windows of Nicole's black Renault with its own chauffeur I caught a glimpse of the Eiffel Tower in the distance. Then we were whizzing along the broad avenues that run alongside the Seine and crossing over the river. I looked out of the window at pink horse-chestnut trees in bloom, and elegant cafés on every corner and felt like I was in a movie. *Paris!*

"This is the Left Bank," Nicole explained. "The artists' side of the city. The most famous names all went to art school here: Matisse, Picasso and Renoir, and Rose of course. That café on your left? Les Deux Magots? It was Rose's favourite. Always filled with painters, talking and eating and drinking."

Nicole saw the worried look on my face.

"Is there something wrong, Maisie?"

"I feel like I'm going to let you down," I said. "I'm not a real artist."

Nicole laughed. "But of course you are! You're the chosen one, Maisie! You follow in the footsteps of the great Rose Bonifait herself. Your scholarship bears her name and her world is now yours. Even the rooms that you will live in while you are here in Paris are the same ones that Rose herself occupied when she attended the school."

A block down from Les Deux Magots café we pulled up outside a branch of the most famous cake shop in Paris, Ladurée. I got out of the car and gazed in through the gilt-trimmed windows of the store at a display of rainbow-coloured macarons, little meringues stacked up as if they were precious jewels. We swept past its pretty windows and went in through the doors of the building, into a tiny foyer, which housed an ancient elevator. Nicole ushered me in and slammed the gold doors closed without waiting for the driver. "He'll follow us up with the bags," she assured me as she pressed the button for the top floor.

The elevator rose and I watched the floor numbers whizz by as we went up, up, up. "The Bonifait corporation owns the entire building," Nicole explained. "Most of the levels are offices these days, but the upper level remains our family home . . ."

The elevator came to a sudden, jerky stop and the doors opened and we stepped out into a grand entrance room with an ornate gold ceiling, brilliant green swirly malachite pillars and cold marble floors. It was so huge our entire apartment back home in Brixton could have fitted into it.

"Come this way. Your rooms are in the east wing," Nicole strode ahead, her boots clacking on the marble floor. "You'll have your own bathroom and a small kitchen, but there is no need to cook. You'll take your meals with me and Françoise in the main dining room."

"Who is Françoise?" I asked.

The answer to the question greeted us in the next room. A girl about my age with flame-coloured hair, who looked very much like Nicole, was lying on a sofa piled high with long-haired caramel Persian cats.

"Maman! You're back!" the girl leapt up from the sofa and the cats yowled in complaint as they were flung off in her wake.

"You must be Maisie!" the girl rushed to me and kissed me on both cheeks.

"You can't imagine how excited I am to have you here." The girl's eyes were bright. "All the other artists who've come to stay have been boring adults. But now we have you, and this is going to be the best summer ever. We can go swimming and have ice creams and . . ."

"Françoise." Nicole rolled her eyes. "Maisie is not here for a play date! She is here to attend art school."

"I know that!" Françoise sniffed. "You don't have to be boring about it, though! She can still eat ice creams, can't she?"

Françoise clutched my arm as if I were about to bolt off. "Come on, let me show you the rooms."

Françoise dragged me away before Nicole could stop

28

her, and we scooted together down the corridors and through a door that led to the east wing. Here, the mood of the apartment changed. No more flashy gold and marble. The room I was standing in now clearly belonged to an artist. The worn parquet floors were spattered with paint. A row of easels in various sizes leant against the wall. Down one wall of the room the windows were almost floor to ceiling, letting in the most amazing light and giving me a view over what seemed to be the whole of Paris. "It's very basic, I know." Françoise was apologetic.

"It's perfect," I said.

"Really?" Françoise wrinkled up her nose. "I find it a bit drab and grubby, but it's good that you like it."

\*\*\*

I phoned Dad before bedtime. I told him I'd arrived safely and that everyone was very nice. I could tell he was trying to keep the conversation light to stop me feeling homesick. Neither of us were used to being apart like this. All my life, apart from one school camp, I'd never been away without Dad. "Good luck for tomorrow, Maisie," he said as he hung up. And those words kept me awake way after midnight as I lay in my bed and looked out of the windows at the Paris roofline under the inky night sky and felt sick to my stomach about my first day at school.

*** 

I should never have brought my own canvas. I realised this as I walked across the cobbled courtyard. No one else was carrying one. At the office of the school administrator, Madame Richard, I sat on the chair and waited with my stupid big canvas and my bag, feeling like a little kid in Year Zero at primary school. Madame Richard opened her door. "Maisie? Here you go!"

I thought she would show me inside and talk to me about the school. I expected at the very least she'd show me where the classroom was! Instead, she just gave me a pink slip of paper and waved me towards classroom 1C!

In the end I found it by myself. Classroom 1C was on the lower level of the building, and the number was written in black on the door.

I could hear the buzz of conversation as the door swung open, but the moment they clapped eyes on me the words froze in the air. Sixteen art students, all of them so old they looked, like, almost twenty or something, stood silently behind their easels and stared straight at me. I have never wanted the ground to open up and swallow me so bad.

"You must be Maisie Thompson?" A bearded man in a dust-brown short-sleeved shirt and black-paint splattered jeans came over and shook my hand. "My name is Augustin. Congratulations on your scholarship."

He said the words in perfectly accented English and then he muttered, "It would be nice if they would consult me in these matters of course . . ."

He said this in English too so I'm sure he meant me to understand him, and the meaning of his words, that he hadn't been the one to select me for the scholarship and perhaps was not entirely happy about it. Certainly it didn't seem like he was congratulating me at all and he definitely seemed disgruntled about having me in his class.

"You may take the easel at the front of the room," Augustin directed.

I felt uneasy. It meant that I would have my back to my classmates and they could look over my shoulder and see what I was doing. The idea that these sophisticated art students could see my work as I was creating it suddenly made me deeply self-conscious.

"I see you have brought your own canvas," Augustin said. "Put it aside as we are working on paper and sketch pads at this point. I don't think we are ready to commit our ideas to canvas for posterity quite yet."

There were sniggers from my classmates. I turned bright red, and stared hard at my shoes. "I haven't brought a sketch pad," I replied.

"Then you can borrow mine for the day," Augustin said.

He handed me the pad, and then he went back to the front of the class and began to shuffle papers on his desk. I stood nervously behind the easel, staring at him until he looked up again.

"Yes?"

"I was just wondering," I said. "What we are drawing?"

There was another snigger from my classmates. Augustin looked imperiously down his nose at me.

"Mademoiselle Thompson," he said. "This is my class, but you have your own mind, do you not? I'm not here to guide your hand. What you decide to draw is up to you."

I wanted to say, well, why did I come all the way to France just so I can stand here with no direction or input then? I could draw by myself at home just as easily. But I got my pencil out and began to sketch. I was thinking about the last series of pictures that I'd done – works based around those big black-and-white cobs who hacked around Hyde Park. I decided to continue with that, and drew from my memory.

Soon, I had the outlines down and I was sketching detail, the tree boughs above them, the riders on their backs. Behind me, the rest of the class were laughing at something. I tried to ignore it, and then the girl right behind me spoke up. My French was poor but I could make out what she was saying – it was something like: "Look, sir. I have my end-of-year assignment completed ready for the auction at Lucie's."

There was laughter from the class as she showed off her drawing. It was a stick-figure pony with a circle for a tummy and four sticks for its legs.

"Stop wasting time, Antoinette," Augustin replied. "Get on with your work."

"Ah, but, sir," Antoinette persisted. "Isn't this all you have to do now to get into the Paris School and the auction too? Draw pictures of pretty ponies!"

There were more giggles until Augustin snapped. "Enough! All of you!"

But it didn't stop. For the rest of the day I could hear them, making little whinnies and clip-clops. It turned out that the auction the girl was talking about was the big deal for the students. Being selected to sell your work at Lucie's was a prestigious achievement for the best pupils at the school. At the end of term, only the superstars of the Paris School would make the cut and be picked. Needless to say, after today I wasn't thinking that short list was going to include me. At the end of class Augustin had looked at my drawing and hadn't uttered a single word.

He hated my work – I could sense it. And the students hated me. So that was it. I had come all the way to Paris to be teased – just as I had been back home – for drawing horses!

***

There was a bath in my private rooms. I love baths and we don't have one at home. That night, I lay back in the tub with my eyes shut tight, and I heard the laughter of Antoinette and her friends in my head and

I felt like no matter what Nicole had said, I was never, ever going to be a real artist. I didn't belong here. I lay there and listened to the tap drip, and then I stretched my hand back to grab the soap and I felt my knuckles rap against the wood panelling of the bathroom wall. It was a hollow sound, an empty clonk. The wall panel wasn't solid. I tested the other panels. The sound was solid. The hollow panel was different from the rest. I knocked my knuckles against it again and this time, the panel twisted and pivoted away. I panicked, thinking I had somehow broken the wall! Then I realised it wasn't broken at all. I had somehow uncovered a secret hidden chamber. A hidey-hole, just big enough to put personal items. I peered in but I couldn't see anything.

I got out of the bath, towelled myself down and went and got my phone. I turned on the torch function and squinted inside the hidey-hole. At first I thought there was nothing inside at all – it looked entirely empty. But then I saw something sitting on the bottom of the cupboard. I picked it up and dusted it off. It was a book, wrapped in an ancient cloth-cover. Inside, where time hadn't faded it, the cloth was dark brown but the exterior had been bleached like bone to grey, and on the front it was imprinted with three dark blood-red gilded letters – MRB. Later, I would discover that they were initials and the M stood for Marie. It was her first name, although no one knew her as Marie; everyone always called her Rose. Rose Bonifait. And the book I had just discovered in the secret chamber that day was her diary.

# CHAPTER 4

## *The Diary of Rose Bonifait*

### *July 4, 1852*

I have spent all morning at the abattoir. You cannot imagine how much it upsets me, but I have to go – it's my duty as an artist to understand the anatomy of the animals that I paint – from their skin to the very core, bone and sinew. It makes me glad every time I visit that I am vegetarian – even though Madame Gris complains so much about how difficult it is to feed me with my fussy, strange ways. One day, she will see. It will be considered normal to do as I do and choose not to eat God's creatures.

This morning it was with the usual sense of dread that I went in. But I steeled myself and I did it, and I stopped myself from gagging. I sat in the corner as the men went about their gruesome task and I drew. I looked at every detail, and I tried to be detached and professional, as if I were, say, a vet or a surgeon. It is easier said than done, however, and two hours later, when I emerged into the sunlight with six sketches in my book, I was shaking and in floods of tears. All I could think to do was to escape the misery of what I had witnessed by doing the one thing in the world that I love more than painting. And so I went to the stables beneath our Parisian city apartment and I saddled Celine.

Of all the horses we own, she is *the one*. No other mare in our stables is as clever as she is, or as kind.

I remember summer holidays at the chateau in Fontainebleau when Mama would put me on terrible Sebastian. That tiny grey pony with the flashing eyes and dainty hooves! Oh, Sebastian – what a terror he was! If you were on his back then his only thought was to get rid of you! His favourite trick was to sweep underneath the boughs of a low-branched tree to knock you off. If this failed then he bucked like a bronco. And if that didn't work he would take himself off into the field and drop to his knees, preparing to roll on top of you! If you didn't leap off his back at this point, he would crush you, and the trick was so effective that he broke the saddle twice before Mama gave up on saddles entirely. After that, she just used a saddle blanket and a surcingle on him to save the expense of buying a new saddle time and again. Sebastian was the closest thing I have ever seen to pure evil and yet, oh how we loved Sebastian! It was only once Mama despaired of his endless naughty antics and realised that despite his diminutive size he might actually do us harm, that she retired him and bought us Celine to ride instead.

So when I say that my education as a horsewoman began with Celine it is true – because all Sebastian taught me was how to jump off very quickly to avoid being squashed.

Celine is the opposite of Sebastian. You could not find a horse more even tempered, sweeter or more compliant. She's almost twenty now – when we first got her she was nine years old, a mare in her prime. Celine is very beautiful, and I know that shouldn't matter, but it does with horses. She's a rich russet chestnut, with a blond mane and tail, deep-brown eyes and clean, slender legs. Her face has a perfect dish – a little Arabian blood saw to that. And the four white socks and the star on her forehead stand out like snow against the burnish of her coat. I have so many drawings of her in my sketch book. She is good at posing. She always pricks her ears forward and arches her neck for me.

When people say that they prefer geldings because mares are moody and ill-tempered, I think to myself – well, you clearly never met my horses. Or me! I am a girl, after all, just like Celine, and I'm always cheerful and in good spirits and both my brothers, Philippe and Dorian, can be very sulky boys indeed! I am a better rider than either of them too, and a better painter. Not that I'm boastful – *no one likes it when girls are proud*. Papa warns me constantly about that. And I reply that no one seems to like it much when girls do anything at all. I am working on solutions to this problem.

Like when the Paris School turned me down because I was a girl. I wasn't foolish enough to try to argue with them that my work was better than any. Instead, I accepted their rejection and I resolved to work harder still. Locked in my room, all I did was paint, night and day. I did not leave the house, save for twice each week, when I would pack up my easel and my paints and I would walk to Hospital Boulevard where the horse markets take place. Here, amongst the chaos, I would set up my equipment and I would focus my eye on the horses. The most amazing creatures went under the hammer at these auction yards. Men would enter leading cavalcades of mares, all rich bays or burnished chestnuts. There were pleasure horses for ladies to ride and work horses for pulling carts. Thick-set grey dappled Percherons and burly Ardennais were very popular and the men who brought them through to the yards for sale would plait their manes with stiff red ribbons and meticulously braid and bind their tails. Their coats shone from being strapped with hay wisps and their hooves were oiled and polished. I know this because I captured every detail on my canvases. I would stay there silent in the corner and paint and paint as the auction was underway until the last lot had been sold and the emptied-out yards stank of dung and cigarettes and sweat.

For three months I worked in this way until I had two paintings that I considered worthy of being submitted to the school. My third and best painting was a work created in the Jardin de Luxembourg, not far from our own stables. It was a portrait of Celine. In this work, I'd painted her side-on, standing in the sunshine dappled by trees. She was staring into the distance, ears pricked and eyes kind. I wasn't entirely satisfied with the work. There was something unnatural about her legs – perhaps the angle of her hocks – legs are fiendishly tricky to do. But all the same, I knew it was a good picture. Her proportions were perfect and the colours and contours were lifelike and shiny. All three paintings were far better than any of those works by the boys who had applied to art school that year. But, don't say that out loud, Rose! Girls are not allowed to be boastful, remember?

Anyway. I didn't. I never boasted about these three paintings. In fact, I didn't mention them to anyone at all. Except to Dorian. He's the middle sibling and only a year older than me, and we've always been thick as thieves. We look alike too; pale and skinny, both with a dark sweep of fringe hiding our blue eyes. Dorian was eight when Mama died. I was seven and I used to cry myself to sleep every night until Papa decided that the two of us should share a room. Dorian moved into the bunk bed above mine and he would sing to me and tell me stories until I slept again.

Anyway, it was to Dorian that I turned to solve my problem with the Paris School. My brother has quite the honest face so he seemed perfect for the trick I had in mind. Together, he and I wrapped the three canvases in soft muslin to protect them, and then Dorian tucked them under his arm and with me trailing behind him we went to the apartments of the Paris School.

Being an artist is in the Bonifait blood. My papa and his father before him both attended the Paris School. So when Dorian went up to the front desk and introduced himself as a Bonifait and asked for an audience with the Directeur, the head of college admissions, Master Demarchelier, was more than willing.

Master Demarchelier didn't so much as glance at me waiting there in my chair as he ushered Dorian into his office. That was fine by me. I sat there outside his rooms in the corridor and while I couldn't hear what was being said behind the closed door, I knew it was going well as they were in there a long while. Eventually my brother emerged, the Directeur with his arm around his shoulder looking most pleased with himself and burbling on about his delight in finding such a gifted pupil just at the eleventh hour when new enrolments for this school year were about to close. He was about to shake hands with Dorian to seal the deal when I leapt forward and pressed my own hand into his in my brother's stead.

"My name is Rose Bonifait," I told him, "and I am the artist who painted these works, not my brother Dorian. So it is I, not Dorian, who will be attending your school."

It was a scandal of course. People are so easily scandalised. That a twelve-year-old girl should be admitted to the Paris School! The master was not best pleased at being tricked. Yet even in his annoyance he had to admit my work was so good he would overlook the naughty ruse and let me in. And so, I became the first-ever girl to attend his college.

From day one at the school they all whispered about me. Nowadays they don't even bother to whisper – they say it straight to my face. You are an impudent young girl and you do not belong here with us, the intellectual elite. It bothers them still more than I really don't care, and I make it so obvious. Yesterday, in class, the Directeur tried to pick at the thread of my temper when he asked me what I thought I was playing at with my ridiculous costume I had taken to wearing.

"I don't know what you mean, sir," I said.

"You keep coming to these classes dressed as a boy," the Directeur pointed out.

I was so sick of trying to paint in my silly lace gowns that for several mornings now, with Dorian's permission, I had raided his wardrobe for his cast-offs. He'd given me some old boiled wool breeches in dark charcoal, a white cotton shirt and a houndstooth waistcoat. I liked the way the wool trousers and the cotton felt against my skin. And, oh, the unbelievable freedom of movement! Dorian gave me jackets too – and socks and ties and it was marvellous to be dressed at last in clothes that were comfortable.

"Mademoiselle Bonifait," the Directeur said to me. "You must dress like a lady to attend the Paris School."

"But, sir," I replied. "I thought ladies weren't allowed to attend the Paris School. And now I am dressed like a boy you do not like that either? You should make up your mind."

Even the boys in class, most of whom hate me for being there, had to laugh at that. As for the Directeur, he huffed that I had better "change my appearance by morning".

Well, that made me so cross I decided I certainly would change it! In the bathroom mirror that night I stared at my reflection and my long, dark ringlet curls, which I usually shaped each evening before bed by wrapping them in brown paper to keep the curl precise. Well, I thought, Monsieur Directeur, you are right. I must change. No more brown paper for me.

I got out the scissors from Mama's old sewing kit. The blades were so sharp that when I ran my finger along to test them, I nearly sliced the tip of my finger clean off. I sheared into my long, dark ringlets and the blade cut through the hair like butter. After I'd shorn them off, I tidied up using a pudding bowl to create a shape.

The pile of hair on the floor beside me looked a bit like a rat scurrying across the floorboards. Then Dorian came in and asked me what on earth I had done.

"I look more like you now, don't you think?" I teased him.

The short cut brings out my eyes, makes the most of my cheekbones. And it will be so practical! No more hair in my eyes when I am trying to paint. I can focus on the work. Anyway, curls never got me anywhere. The boys at the school seldom even acknowledge that I am alive, and the only other places I ever go are the auction yards and the abattoir, and curls are no use to me there either.

Back to the abattoir. As I said, I was there this morning. I had skipped my lesson at school – I suddenly didn't feel like facing the Directeur with my new hair. His endless, painful discussions about the failings of my gender were irritating me too much for me to hold my tongue, and going instead to a place where they slaughter animals felt like a pleasant change of pace.

I'm being horrible. Truly, it is never fun to go to the abattoir. This morning, though, dealing with what I saw in that slaughter chamber upset me even more than usual, and I had a feeling of being deeply heartbroken when I emerged. As I saddled Celine, I wondered whether the stench of the place clung to me in some way because the mare skipped and danced as I tacked her up, but she settled when I mounted, and we rode out across the gravel of the forecourt of the stables and down the avenues to the park.

The Jardin de Luxembourg is still my favourite place in the world. Winding bridle paths meander between trees and around the great lake, and there is a sense of wildness to the place so that you can scarcely believe you are in the city. One day I even spied deer bounding through the forest as I rode.

Before Mama got sick, we would ride there together, and she would point out things and make me practise my English. *L'oiseau is bird. L'arbre is tree. Jardin is garden.* I chanted these words to myself today as I rode the bridle paths with Celine and then cantered my mare through the trees, watching the dappled late-afternoon light of Paris growing rose-pink as the evening closed in on us. By the time I returned Celine to her stall that evening, I had made my mind up about two things.

The first was that, no matter what happened to me in my life, I would always love horses.

The second thing I decided was perhaps more important. Until now, I have been quiet. I have apologised for my gender and been happy to let men consider me to be the weaker sex, have allowed them to make decisions that are unfair and unequal. But the Directeur's silly fuss about something as pointless as my style of dress has strengthened my ambition, has turned my will to steel.

No matter what Papa says about the importance of girls being modest and demure, I know I will never be these things and I refuse to be considered less than a man. Because the second thing that I decided today when I was out riding is that I am going to be the greatest artist in the world. That is my plan – and when I make my mind up, I do not fail.

## Chapter 5

## *The Horse Guards*

By the time I stopped reading Rose's diary the bath-water had gone cold and my toes had turned wrinkly. Wiping my hands on my towel to keep the pages from getting damp, I carefully put the book back into the hidey-hole. That secret chamber was actually quite easy to manipulate now that I knew how. All I had to do was tap hard to pivot the false panel and it would open to the dark space beyond where the diary had been concealed, undiscovered for a hundred and fifty years.

I didn't doubt that it was real; that what I'd held in my hands was the actual journal of Rose Bonifait. There was one thing puzzling me, though. How come the diary was in English? The answer, by chance, came

49

to me in a conversation with Nicole at breakfast the next morning.

"I was wondering," I said, as she served me up brioche and jam and a big mug of hot chocolate. "Why did Rose choose to offer this scholarship to a pupil from England?"

"But I thought you knew?" Nicole was surprised. "Rose herself was English on her mother's side. Eleanor Claridge arrived from London at the age of eighteen to study in Paris in 1830. Her parents intended her to become a refined lady who would return to them with a rounded education and sophisticated manner. But instead, the young Eleanor met Rose's father, Jacques Bonifait. It was a whirlwind romance, nobody approved, but they got married regardless and Madame Eleanor Bonifait never left France again. She died when Rose was only seven."

And now it all made sense to me. In the diary Rose had spoken of her mother teaching her English in the park. So Rose had been fluent in two languages! And after her mother died, what better way to keep her diary secret than to write in a tongue that no one else in the household could speak?

I didn't tell Nicole about finding the diary. Or

50

Françoise either. I felt so guilty, but I needed time to think about what to do with it. In my hands that diary felt almost like a portal to another time. I was consumed by Rose's story and the power of the secrets held in that journal. I felt like she would have wanted me to see it, but would she have wanted her innermost thoughts shared with the rest of the world? Weirdly, that felt like a betrayal of her confidence. And so I was torn over my loyalty to my guardian, Nicole, and my bond to my benefactor, Rose, a girl who had been dead now for a hundred and fifty years. All I knew was that once I handed the diary over to Nicole, there would be no going back. The book would become an artefact to be pored over by intellectuals and historians. But in my hands it was alive somehow, and so was Rose.

It made me feel better, too, knowing that Rose had felt like an outsider at the Paris art school just like me. If she could rise above it to become great, then so would I.

Augustin did not even look at me when I entered the classroom that morning. The other students all talked amongst themselves. Sure, maybe they thought it wasn't worth trying to talk to me, but even so they could have at least acknowledged my presence with a *bonjour* or something, right? Anyway, without a word from anyone I took up the same place at the easel where I had been sketching the day before and began to work.

I kept my head down and focused on my picture. The drawing was really taking shape now. I was filling in the details on the black-and-white cobs, working up the textures of their manes, the ripples of their muscles and the reflections on their coats of the dappled light through the overhanging tree boughs. Now, as they became more defined on my sketch pad, I found my own focus becoming more intense. With each line and smudge I was bringing them alive, pressing hard against the paper with the charcoal to get the dark bits I needed, then going back over to rework the charcoal, smudging it and rubbing out areas to create shade and light. I was working from fiction, and yet it felt I'd recreated a scene that was so real, if you gave it a very quick glance it almost looked like a photograph.

I was so engrossed that at one point I looked up at the clock and saw that hours had passed! Finally, I felt that I had the picture just as I wanted it, and as chance would have it, at exactly the same moment Augustin was telling us that our time was up and commanding that we put down our paintbrushes and pencils. I watched him walk around the room gathering up the work, peeling the top page from our sketch books so that soon he had all of our drawings, including mine. He took the stack back to the front of the classroom and, using sticky tape, he quickly stuck them up on the classroom wall so that we could all see them lined up in two rows.

It was a shock. All this time, I had been so focused on my own work, I hadn't cast a glance at the other easels. Now, displayed like this, I could see that the other sixteen pictures on the wall were nothing like mine. They weren't even pictures – well, not like I thought of a picture. I've never wanted to make modern art, and to me these pictures were all kind of weird. Some of them were no more than splodges, smears and blobs. Others were just bold words scrawled in French. One picture was nothing more than three spindly lines with a splodge on top and it was this one that Augustin actually singled out first to discuss with the class.

"Now here is a composition that speaks to me!" he enthused. "When I look at this work I think 'Yes! This is what is modern now!' This is art that confronts the viewer, and asks them to question: what is life? What does it all mean?"

I was boggling at this. As far as I could see all we were staring at here was a couple of wiggly lines and a blob. Was that a commentary on life? Apparently so, because Augustin didn't stop! He raved on about it for ages in a way that seemed positively bonkers and then . . . embarrassingly, he went straight over to my work next.

I already had this sick feeling in my gut before he spoke a word. I mean, if he thought the dumb squiggles were "modern" and "confronting" then how could he possibly like my picture too? There was a part of me though that held out hope all the same, that maybe he would find himself bowled over by my skill. After all, hadn't I won a scholarship that got me into this place? They had brought me here from England for this. That had to mean I was talented, right? And then Augustin opened his mouth and all my hope was gone.

"We come now to a picture of horses," Augustin said. "And horses are powerful creatures, are they not? But do you feel their power? Do you hear their hooves? Do you smell their earthy dung or their sweet, honeysuckle breath? No. You do not. Because this is a picture with no soul. Yes, there is some technique. But what does this matter if the art fails to captivate me? A picture like this is a hollow vessel. This is not art. This is just drawing. And so, for me, it ultimately disappoints."

And that was it! In front of everyone, just like that, he had ripped my heart out. And without even looking at me, that was it; his criticism was done. Augustin moved on to the next picture and now he was gushing once again over some blobs and squares, talking about the magnificence of their colours and clever ideas and the students were all chiming in with their thoughts, and meanwhile I was just left standing there, shaking behind my easel, totally broken into bits.

No one else seemed to bat an eyelid at his cruelty. They all just carried on listening to him as he bleated on about heart and passion and who cares what else. And I stood there, and I felt myself consumed by how much I despised this man for ripping apart my work like that. Yes, I was crying a little, but not big tears, and not because I was sad. I was angry. By the time Augustin had been through all the works – mine was not the only one he hated, but it was undoubtedly the one he hated most – and he'd told us we could take a break for lunch, I had decided I needed to talk to him.

I waited until the rest of the class had gone out and then I went over to his desk. The blood was still pulsing at my temples, making a whooshing noise in my ears.

"Augustin?"

He turned around to me. He looked completely blank, as if he had no idea why I would want to talk to him.

"I . . ." I didn't know how to begin. "You seem to really hate my work," I said. "I'm just wondering if there's even any point in me coming back here tomorrow."

Augustin looked hard at me, saw that I'd been crying.

"I don't hate your work, Maisie," he said. "It inspires no feelings in me at all; that is the problem. I look at your 'art' and I feel nothing. It is old-fashioned, meaningless and dated. Pictures of horses? What does that say to me about modern life, about the world we live in now? No. I will not sugar-coat it for you just because you are younger than the others. You have technique, it is true, but it is worthless unless you produce work that sparks emotion, that speaks from your heart and soul. This school is about work that feels fresh and avant-garde – art that shocks with its spirit and courage. This is what a real artist does, Maisie. If you think you will make it through the Paris School with an A-grade by drawing pretty ponies, then you are wasting all of our time."

And with that, Augustin turned his back on me and walked out of the room.

I stood at the front of the class after he'd gone, and I stared at my picture. Really? Was it so very bad? The horses were accurate enough. I walked back and forth examining the other pictures stuck to the wall, looking hard at the other works, the ones that he'd singled out as his favourites. He liked their modernism, their daring. If I put my own wounded feelings aside, perhaps I could see a little of what he saw, but even if I did see it, I knew I couldn't imitate it. If I'd tried to copy, then my work would have even less heart than Augustin claimed it did now. I couldn't do some ridiculous mimicry of the scribbles and blobs that I saw before me. All I'd ever wanted to do was to paint horses. Unfashionable, dated, what was the other word he said? Oh yes, meaningless. Meaningless horses.

There was a whole afternoon of class still to come, but what was the point in sticking around? Augustin hated my work, and I hated being here, and right now all I could think was that this whole art school thing had been a stupid, crazy mistake and all I wanted was to go home.

I was crying again by the time I left the school grounds. I ran out on to the street and I was wiping my eyes as I went round the corner, which is kind of an excuse, but not really, because even with blurred vision you would think I would be able to see a horse right in front of me.

I ran straight into him. Like, I know people say that, but I did. Smack into his forelegs – it was like crashing into a tree. He was enormous! Almost seventeen hands and jet black, and when I looked up it was like looking up at a mountain, that huge, muscular slab of a neck, thick shoulders and the massive legs. I staggered back and said, "Sorry!" – which was funny when I thought about it later, apologising to a horse's legs. The horse, he didn't even flinch. Didn't even move a muscle. Police horses are trained to be unflappable.

"*Son nom est Claude,*" the policeman who had been mounted on his back told me after he'd leapt down to pick me up off the ground.

"*En anglais?*" I said.

"Ah," the gendarme smiled. "You are English? *Bien.* I speak it well. All I was saying is that his name is

Claude. If you like, you can stroke his muzzle. He is very friendly. Don't be afraid."

"I'm not," I said. "I'm not scared of horses."

"*Bien*," the policeman said. "So, you like horses? What is your name?"

"Maisie," I said.

"Well, Maisie, would you like to meet Claude's friends? We're just on our way back to the Célestins Quarter, the police-horse city stables where he lives. Come with us if you want? It's almost parade time."

They always say that you shouldn't talk to strangers. But this stranger was a policeman, and they also say you should find one if you need help. So I figured it was OK to go. And it turned out we weren't going far. All this time I had been so close to horses – just one street up from the art school were the high, baroque iron gates of the Célestins. Tourists were queueing outside, waiting to come in to see the afternoon display of the guards on horseback, and I thought the policeman might leave me there to wait with them, but he called to me to stay at his side and I walked through the gates as if I was being escorted by Claude, until I was in the central courtyard of the grand enclosure with buildings on every side. Here, gravelled paths were bordered by neatly clipped topiary hedges and a sand arena for the display stood at the centre. I followed around the perimeter of the arena alongside Claude, then through the stone arch of the main stable blocks. I was stunned at how many stalls there were. There must have been more than a hundred horses living here! The cobbled corridors echoed with the sounds of men laughing and joking as they saddled their horses ready for the show. Their horses looked almost identical, rich golden chestnuts, as shiny and burnished as a copper coin.

"Hey, Oscar!" One of the other guards spoke to Claude's rider. "You have a young friend?"

"This is Maisie," Oscar called back. "She's come to watch you perform, so you'd better not mess it up like you usually do, Alexandre!"

There was a lot of laughter from the others at this. They were all mounting now, and from another wing of the stables came still more horses, grey ones this time. They were very elegant and dressed in cavalry saddle blankets across their dappled backs. They had long free-flowing manes and sooty leg-stockings and dark eyes and muzzles. As I watched them take their places, ready to perform, the tourists gathered in the courtyard on the seats waiting for them to begin. I breathed it all in, the sounds and the smells and the sense of pure heaven to be in such a place. And when Claude took his place at the front of the parade and held me with his dark and intense gaze, I felt myself become lost in the mysteries hidden in those deep, black eyes of his. He was so beautiful, so powerful and so gentle at the same time. Of all the horses here at the Célestins, there was something special about him. He was the most noble horse I had ever seen. And at that moment, although I didn't realise it yet, in the realms of the Célestins Garde, I had found what every artist needs. As Rose explained to me later in the diary, I had discovered something in Claude. He was to become my muse.

CHAPTER 6

## *The Stag and the Pheasant*

*August 24, 1852*

Papa says all great artists have a muse: someone that symbolises ultimate beauty for them and inspires them to feel the emotions they need to create their art. Horses are my muse. Every day I find something new in them that I want to capture. Until now, my muse had always been Celine, but Papa forced me to leave the mare behind in the city when we left to spend the summer at Fontainebleau. Luckily our chateau here in the country has a stable full of horses I can use as my models if need be.

My routine at Fontainebleau is no different to life at home. All I do is paint. For two weeks, I have been cooped up in my room with my work, creating a picture that expressed my torment after visiting the abattoir. The picture I've painted is of a horse being attacked by a lion. Of course, I live in Paris, so I've never witnessed that first hand. Even here in Fontainebleau, where the oak forests have bears and deer and wild boar hidden in their darkest depths, there are no lions. There is a stuffed lion in one of the museums in Paris, though, and I've seen him up close. I spent a whole day there before we left for Fontainebleau, sitting at his feet and drawing him, noting particulars like the texture of his fur, the shagginess of his mane. These sketches I have now reworked into my painting to show the great beast leaping through the air and gouging his claws into the back of a wild horse.

The horse in this painting is based on a young colt here at Fontainebleau. There was a thunderstorm one afternoon, and I watched this bay colt running wild as the lightning struck, the way he tossed his mane in fear and the whites of his eyes gleaming. That is what I have tried to capture here in the painting, with the sinew and flesh from the abattoir to make my work realistic. I want to feel as if the horse in my painting is truly alive.

This is my assignment for school this term, and as soon as I'm done with it, as a reward, Papa says he will take me hunting. The horses we keep in the stables here at our chateau are very good, and the forests are perfect for riding. This will be my first time riding out with the hounds. I'm very excited. But first I must finish the work. Madame Gris knocks on my door every few hours with a tray of food. There's still more to be done before the painting is finished, but the light is fading now, so I will paint by gaslight for a while and then I'll sleep, and in the morning I'll begin again. Everyone envies the artist's life, but this is the part they don't see. I should be on holiday, picking wildflowers and berries and playing in the gardens, but instead I do nothing but work, work, work. Still, it will be worth it, if the work is good enough.

*August 26, 1852*

The work is dreadful. I don't know why. The paint sits on the canvas in a way that should please me, but it is horrible. It has no soul. I give up. I'm going out hunting.

I hate my father, and Philippe too. They are pure evil. Yesterday, I went out hunting, which was supposed to be my treat for finishing my painting. A painting which I haven't finished, as it happens, because it is too awful, but that is not the point. I was so fed up with it all, I pushed the easel aside and I joined the hunting party, hoping the fresh forest air would clear my head and do me good, perhaps.

There were eight of us riding out yesterday. My family – Papa and Philippe and Dorian and myself – made four, plus the duc of the estate next door and his huntsmen made us eight.

We set off at a canter through the forests following after the hounds – there were six of these and they were terrible howlers, baying and carousing at the merest provocation as they ran ahead. I had been given a big, heavy roan draught horse that was a little too strong and too big for me, so I was mostly concentrating on keeping him back as he fought to get to the front. Horses in a large group will often get hot and uncontrollable, and he was being very headstrong, pulling hard on the reins and pushing off his hocks to leap forward in ridiculous bounds, fretting at the bit. My entire focus had become staying in the saddle and not being tossed to the ground. I haven't fallen off a horse in a very long time, not since I was perhaps seven years old, and I didn't want to break my record now.

At the sound of the horn, I knew the master upfront had sighted a stag, and now we were galloping and the horses were fighting to take the lead and it was bedlam. The tracks soon narrowed – stags do not care to stick to the paths – and we began to ride in single file, into the very heart of the forest. As the trees closed in, I stayed low on my horse's neck to avoid being hit by a bough, and at the same time I tried to keep my weight in my heels and my thighs gripped tight. The roan, despite his speed, was spooking constantly at every leaf that fluttered, and I thought that any minute he might veer in either direction and I would be flung to the ground. There was no time to think about anything except for hanging on for dear life, and there was certainly no way of stopping. If I had tried to pull the roan up, or to turn him to go back and away from the others, he would have mutinied and bucked or reared, and that would have been the end of me. All I could do was keep my seat and stay with the hunt.

Then there was a moment where the roan stopped

pulling at the reins and slowed a little, and suddenly it was magical and we were riding onwards, all of us in unison through the trees, the lilt of the horn calling us forward and the wind smacking my cheeks and blowing back my hair. I felt free and at one with nature and then . . . then I heard the arrows being loosed, and there was a guttural cry of pain so hideous and heartbreaking it took me straight back to the abattoir. And we were pulling to a halt and my horse was heaving and twitching because, there in front of us on the ground, flailing about, panting and wild-eyed, was the stag.

I can see that I seem childish now, but truly I had never thought about what would happen when we caught him. I just saw the hunt as a chance to ride out through the wilds. Now, I saw it for what it was – the ruthless running down and murdering of a magnificent beast.

I threw myself down from my horse's back and began to try and work one of the arrows out that had pierced the deer.

"Rose!" My father was shocked. "Move away! You'll get injured."

"But we have to help him!" I begged Papa.

"It's too late for that," my father said. "Now move! You are ruining the shot."

I looked up and saw my papa sitting on his horse, crossbow drawn. He had his sights set square at me. Which was to say, they were set on the deer and I was in the line of death.

Behind me, the stag was breathing in a laboured fashion. I looked at his glassy eyes, the blood on his coat where the arrows that had taken him down were embedded deep. I stepped aside and let my father take the final shot.

He was always going to die. I know that. Those first arrows had already done the damage before I'd stepped aside and let my papa end it all. If I'd refused to move, I would have just made his suffering last longer. I told myself all of this on the long ride home through the forest. We went slowly on the way back because we had the stag with us, slung over the front of one of the duc's horses, while his huntsman walked alongside on foot leading the horse.

Last night, it was venison for dinner. I told Papa I would rather starve to death, and he said that was fine by him and sent me to my room. Here, I felt the injustice and horror of the day well up inside me, and I began to rework the painting – the one of the horse and the lion. I could see now where I had gone wrong. Until this moment, I had captured only the pain of the horse, but now I was trying to show the intensity of the struggle that existed for both the hunter and his prey. After all, if the lion didn't kill he would starve to death. The same was not true for us today when my father shot the stag – we have a kitchen full of food!

I think the revisions are successful enough for me to pass my end of term. Tomorrow we go back to Paris. Next week I'm back at school. I look forward to having the smell of oil paint on my hands once more instead of blood. I'm going riding in the morning before we leave. I shall take the roan and go alone.

*August 31, 1852*

I did not anticipate that the roan would be no better behaved alone than he was in company. From the moment we departed the yard he was atrocious, shaking his head and pulling the reins again and again, reefing until my fingers were raw, even through the gloves that I was wearing, and my nerves were frazzled from constantly fighting his urges to bolt with me. He trotted and sidestepped through the forest like a crab, constantly looking this way and that with his eyes on stalks and spooking at anything and everything on the ground. A leaf! A fallen bough! A squirrel! He was driving me demented and the ride was not in any way enjoyable, and after half an hour of this nonsense I had decided to turn for home when it happened.

The pheasant was right underneath his hooves when it flew up and the racket the bird made with its wing beats and the flash of rainbow feathers would have frightened even the most sensible horse. The roan went straight up. I remember thinking that I should try to stay on board, even though he was right up on his hind legs, that it would be safer to remain on his back than to fall and be trodden on. And then there was this sickening lurch and I felt gravity working in all the wrong directions and he was coming over backwards on top of me as we fell down to the ground. And then everything turned black.

When I woke again, it was black still. Night had fallen, and I was so cold. The roan was gone. As it turned out, it would be him that saved me from dying out there. The horse had bolted straight for home, and the stable boy had found him trotting about the yard and had realised I must have fallen. When I hadn't come home by the afternoon, a search party was sent out. In the darkness I saw their lanterns and I called out. I was shocked at how reedy and thin my voice was, as if the strength had ebbed from me. In its place, there was blind terror. Because, I couldn't go to them. They would have to come to my voice, they would have to find me. And that was what terrified me. The fact that I couldn't move.

When they found me, I told them my legs wouldn't behave and insisted that I was certain they were still sticking up in the air. I don't remember this at all. I just remember them picking me up, and at that moment realising that it was not just the cold that had made me numb. I literally could not feel anything at all from the waist down.

They threw me over the back of one of the huntsmen's horses to get me home. What else could they do? I couldn't sit up. I couldn't ride. I lay there, spread across with my limbs dangling, just as the dead stag had done a few days before. I came into the yard like this and my papa tore those grooms to shreds for treating me as if I were a sack of potatoes to be flung about. Gently, he lifted me down and carried me to the grand upstairs room with the windows that looked out over the court-yard. Then he ordered a bed warmer to be prepared even though it was summer and there were no hot coals in the fireplace to use for such things. He barked at the grooms to ride out and fetch the doctor to come and examine me, threatening Madame Gris with the guillotine if she didn't hurry herself to bring me soup and warm bread to fill my stomach.

The doctor arrived in the depth of the night. He examined me. Asked me if I could feel my arms and hands – I could. And my legs? I could not.

He pressed my toes, massaged my calves, and then, using a needle that he produced from his black bag, he pricked the tip into my toes one by one.

Any sensation at all? Nothing I said. And again. And again. Both sets of toes, and the soles of my feet. And now further up my legs and it was amazing to me, to see the pin prick my skin until my blood was drawn to the surface in tiny red flecks. I felt nothing at all.

Later, after he had gone. I tried it myself. I had slipped a needle out of his black bag without his noticing and I tested just as he had done. Nothing. In the end, in desperation, I stabbed the needle so deep into my leg it should have made me scream. Instead, I lay and sobbed. I cannot move my legs. The doctor wouldn't talk to me, but I heard him. I heard what he said to my father in the hallway as he left this morning when he had come to check my progress and found me the same as the days before. He whispered his prognosis, but my ears are not broken, just my back. The doctor says that I am paralysed from the waist down. He says he is quite certain. The damage to my spine is absolute. I will never walk again.

## CHAPTER 7

# *The Wheelchair Mystery*

I am sure that the doctor is wrong. Rose is going to recover. She is not much older than me, and she has yet to paint her greatest works. Doctors make mistakes about things. I saw a woman come out of a coma once on *Grey's Anatomy,* and no one was expecting it, so it happens.

Today, as I walked across the cobblestones to get to class, I thought about what life would be like without my legs. If I couldn't stand at my easel then I couldn't paint. Mind you, Augustin thinks I'm a useless artist anyway. He hasn't said a kind word to me. I thought he might try to encourage me after being so brutal about my work last week, but no.

In class I've continued to try to rework the sketch as

a painting, to give it the soul he keeps telling me it needs to have. All I've managed to do is make it overwrought and now the paint is so thick and gloopy it won't dry.

After school today I couldn't face going home. I walked out of the gates and went left, heading down the avenue to the Célestins Guards' quarters.

The guard on the gate gave me a smile. "You're Oscar's little friend, aren't you?" He raised the barrier. "He said you might be back."

I couldn't believe he'd just let me in like that. I felt my heart racing as I walked across the courtyard. And then I got to Claude's stall and found it empty, and all the excitement drained out of me.

"They're out on patrol."

It was Alexandre. He was standing behind me in the corridor dressed in his police uniform, the navy jodhpurs and long black boots with a tight navy polo shirt.

"You're looking for Claude, yes?" he asked me. "He is out on duty at the moment, him and Oscar. Their shift finishes in half an hour – wait for them in the gardens if you want."

"Can I wait here?" I asked.

"Sure," Alexandre said. "You know, if you wanted to make yourself useful, you could even muck out his stall?"

"I don't know how," I said. When he looked oddly at me, I added, "I'm from Brixton." Which I thought explained it.

"Brixton?" Alexandre looked puzzled, as though he didn't know what I was talking about. "I'm not suggesting you do brain surgery." Alexandre shrugged. "You get a pitchfork and a wheelbarrow. You pick up the dung. That's all there is to it. You don't need an art school education for this, I don't think."

Oscar must have told him about me being at art school. We'd talked about why I was in Paris the other day. I had hung around in the courtyard after the show was over and Oscar had let me help as he had unsaddled Claude. We'd talked a lot that day.

"It's good for me to talk with you," Oscar had said. "I like to practise my English."

"Your English is already good," I'd said. I'd noticed though that sometimes he would say strange words like, "ten-four" and "Roger that."

"I grew up watching lots of American cop shows when I was a kid." Oscar smiled. "So I speak American a bit."

We talked then about how Oscar had grown up always wanting to be a policeman. "I was an ordinary police officer, you know?" he said. "Then I was hand-picked for the Célestins."

I had asked Nicole about the Célestins. She said they were a little like the British mounted police, but also like the Queen's Guard who rode in parades in London. I thought it would be amazing, to have a job riding horses, and I'd assumed Oscar had been a rider before he came here, but he wasn't.

"I had never been a rider, but when I became a policeman I found it so dull. I thought it would be exciting – catching robbers, car chases. It turns out being a gendarme in the French police is mostly paper-work. Very boring. So I applied to the Célestins. They taught me to ride."

"I think I'd like your job," I said, "riding horses all day for work."

"It's pretty good," Oscar agreed. He stroked Claude's muzzle. "To be paid money to be with your best friend on the streets of Paris every day. There are worse jobs."

He smiled at me. "But you, Maisie, you already have a future career. You are at the Paris School. Fame and fortune as an artist are bound to follow."

"Not if my work sucks as much as Augustin thinks it does," I said.

"Does it matter what he thinks?" Oscar replied.

"Augustin has the final say about which paintings are chosen for the art school auction night at Lucie's," I said. "If I don't get selected, that's kind of like failing."

"And he doesn't like your work?"

I shook my head. "He thinks I'm old-fashioned and I lack emotional depth. Although his idea of 'deep' is stupid modern art that is all squiggles and blobs."

"I would rather have a horse on my wall than a blob." Oscar frowned.

"It was easier at home," I said. "I could go to Hyde Park and set up my easel and paint the horses there."

"You can do the same here," Oscar said. "If you want. Come and paint Claude any time you like. He struggles with life here sometimes. He is happy when he's out working on the streets, but he gets bored and misses human company when he's confined to his stall. If you visited him he would love to model for you."

As if to prove this, Claude had pricked his ears forward and struck a pose.

"See!" Oscar smiled. "He's a natural! Come and paint him anytime."

\*\*\*

Did Oscar really expect me to take him up on the offer or was he just being kind? I filled up the wheelbarrow with dung while I waited for them to return. If I could make myself useful at the yard, perhaps it would feel less like he was doing me a favour.

Alexandre returned when my barrow was full and directed me where to dump it on the dung heap out the back of the yards. He showed me the pile of fresh sawdust too, and I took a barrowload of it back with me to the stall. I was spreading it on the floor when there was the chime of horseshoes on cobbles as the officers came back from their afternoon patrol. I came out into the corridor to see Oscar dismounting and leading Claude in through the courtyard.

Claude gave a nicker at the sight of me. I found it very heartwarming that he'd remembered me, and Oscar smiled and waved. "Maisie!"

He seemed genuinely pleased to see me.

"You've brought your easel, I hope?" he asked.

"Just my sketch book," I said.

"*Bien*. Well, you'll have to give us a few minutes. I need to wash Claude down before he goes into his stall."

"I can help?" I offered.

"Do you remember what the halter looks like?" Oscar asked me.

"It's the thing you stick on his head to tie him up, yeah?"

Oscar nodded. "Go grab it for me from the tack room. His section will have his name on it – you'll find it."

I got the halter and came back and Oscar slipped the saddle, martingale and bridle off – he named them all for me as he worked – and put the halter on. Then he handed me the lead rope and showed me how to lead Claude. "Always stand on the left hand at his shoulder." And I walked Claude over to the wash-down bays and Oscar showed me how to tie him off with a slipknot and how to hose him. It was a bit like watering the garden.

"Don't be afraid to wash his face," Oscar told me. "He loves the water."

When I turned the hose on his head Claude flattened his ears a bit, but he seemed to enjoy it. The water had turned him glistening black. He looked so sleek in the sunlight, shining and wet, his eyes dewy. As Oscar walked him back to his stall I ran ahead and got my sketch pad out.

Oscar turned him loose in the box without his halter

and went to clean his tack and I began to draw. It was very different to how I had sketched horses in the past. Claude was right there next to me now, so I could really capture every detail of his face. I didn't bother with the rest of his body. Instead I just drew the head. I was trying to capture the tiny details, like the whiskers on his damp muzzle and the way his long, thick eyelashes trimmed his coal-black eyes, as if he were a film star. Oscar didn't interrupt me as I worked. He must have gone to join the other guards – I could hear voices in the corridor from time to time. It was getting dark when at last he returned to the stall with Claude's feed – Claude whinnied vigorously at this. Oscar put the feed in the wall bin, strapped up the haynet full of hay, then smiled at me and said, "Hometime."

At the gates he offered to walk me home.

"I'm OK," I insisted. But Oscar laughed and said, "I am offering you a police escort." So I said yes and he walked me to the apartment door. It was dark by now, but the street lamps made everything look pretty, and the macaron shop had the windows all lit up so that the tiny cakes looked like colourful sparkling jewels.

Françoise was lying on the velvet sofa in the living room under a pile of cats.

"You're home!" she said. "At last! Maman! She's back! We can have dinner!"

Nicole burst out from the kitchen, looking quite relieved to see me. "I was about to phone the school and ask whether you were there," she said.

"I was at the Célestins again," I said. "I'm sorry. I should have asked first."

"I don't mind that you go there. Just text me, perhaps? Let me know next time?" Nicole said. "Otherwise your dinner will be overcooked!"

"She's English, Maman," Françoise rolled her eyes. "They like their food overcooked."

I took the insult with a smile. But when Nicole asked me how I liked my steak I lied and said I would have it rare just to prove Françoise wrong. It was all bloody inside. I thought about Rose, how she refused to eat meat.

"Is there something wrong with your meal?" Nicole asked me.

"I . . . I'm a vegetarian," I said suddenly. The words surprised even me.

"Oh." Nicole seemed quite taken aback. "I should have asked. Now I feel dreadful."

"It's fine," I said.

Nicole didn't seem cross, just confused. She picked up the plate with the rare steak. "Let me find you something else. Do you eat cheese? You're not vegan?"

I didn't even know what vegan meant. "I eat cheese," I said.

Nicole returned with some crusty baguette and cheeses and a green salad. It was really good.

"How long have you been a vegetarian, Maisie?" She asked.

"Since today," I had to admit. The look she gave me made it clear that now she thought I was being difficult and, possibly, a little bit nuts.

"It's because of Rose," I said. "She loved animals so she didn't eat them, and it's inspired me, I guess."

"Was she a vegetarian?" Nicole said. "How do you know? What makes you think so?"

I realised then that I still hadn't told them about the diary. "I . . . umm . . . I think I read it somewhere."

"Did you?" Nicole said. "That is so interesting. I would love it if you could recall where you read about her. You know there is so very little historical information about Rose Bonifait. Renoir, Picasso, Matisse, all these male artists had biographies written about them and their work. But Rose was a woman artist in a male-dominated world, and at the time they did not regard her as significant, not the way we know her to be today. So we know virtually nothing about her life. I did not know, for instance, that she was a vegetarian."

"Did you know that she was crippled?"

The words came tumbling out of my mouth before my brain could put the brakes on and stop them. Nicole looked at me, totally stunned.

"There have long been rumours of an accident, a terrible horse fall. But nothing concrete. Is this what you are you talking about?"

"Yes!" I could feel my heart pounding. I had to be careful what I said. How could I possibly know such things unless I had the diary in my possession. And I didn't want to give her the diary, not yet. And so I bare-face lied. "I think I read it in an art book at the college."

Nicole frowned. "I should like to know which book. And when was this fall? What year? Do you recall?"

I did recall. There had been a date at the top of the diary entry. August 1852.

"The year of the accident was 1852," I said.

Nicole's frown deepened. "It is not possible. Are you certain?"

"I think so," I said. I knew so. But Nicole shook her head doubtfully

"Come with me," she said.

We walked out of the dining room and down the hallway.

"In 1856," Nicole said as she led me on, "Rose had left Paris behind. We don't know why. She was living in the Camargue by then, and there is a date-stamped photograph of her from that time. It hangs by the elevator in the entrance – you probably did not see it. Come and look at it now."

I followed her, thinking that if the diary entry where Rose's back had been broken was from 1852 and the photo had been taken two years later and the doctor was right about Rose being paralysed, then surely she was already in a wheelchair?

When Nicole, Françoise and I walked into the entranceway, I realised I hadn't seen the photograph because it was tucked around the corner in the alcove by the window and shadowed by a large houseplant with gigantic green leaves that matched the malachite pillars.

"There," Nicole said. "That is Rose Bonifait in the photograph."

Now as I looked at it, I couldn't believe my eyes. The photograph was a black-and-white print, taken outdoors. It was a spooky, almost ghostly image, of an old French country house, the sky above all dark and ominous. It looked like a storm was coming. But what truly left me startled about the photograph was the girl in the picture, who must have been Rose herself. She did not look injured in any way. She was not sitting in a wheelchair. She was sitting astride a big grey horse.

"The horse, I believe, is a Camarguaise, a wild thing," Nicole at my shoulder breathed to me. "They say Rose was the only one who rode him as no one else could."

"That's impossible . . ." I began. But then I knew I couldn't say more. Was the diary itself a lie? A fake? That made no sense.

"What happened to you?" I murmured to the photograph. But Rose Bonifait did not reply.

CHAPTER 8

## *I Hate Paris in the Springtime*

*November 23, 1852*

Madame Gris has just left my room after giving me a lecture about my life. She walked in here and pulled back my curtains and proclaimed that it was a lovely day and the tulips were in bloom and people were promenading in the Place des Vosges.

"And you lie here in this pit of darkness," she scolded, tying the curtains back, despite my protests that the sunlight hurt my eyes. "You refuse to eat. You won't even get out of bed! I have had enough of your moping, Rose. You must accept what has happened. There is still so much to enjoy in life!"

I lost my temper at her. "Shall I get up then and take a walk in the park?" I snarled. And I threw the bedclothes back, exposing my pale, skinny legs. It is shocking how lifeless my muscles have become, wasted away from disuse in the months since the fall.

"You think I don't want to promenade?" I shouted. "Or ride Celine? Or paint? These things were all I lived for! What am I living for now, Madame? Tell me! Then I will get out of bed and go and see your stupid tulips!"

Then I threw a shoe at her, and she went back out of my door and left me alone.

I don't know what the shoe was even doing there. I seldom wear shoes now. What use are they when my feet never touch the ground? I have my wheelchair parked beside the bed and I can slide myself on to it, and use my hands to push myself by the wheels, but this apartment is not built for wheelchairs and I get stuck all the time in doorways and then I have to shriek for Madame Gris to come and get me free again. She is fed up with me and my miserableness. But I don't care. I don't care about anything any more since the fall. I'm not getting out of bed for some ridiculous flowers.

## November 30, 1852

Dorian took me down to the stables today in my wheelchair. He had convinced me we were just going for a short walk, but then he turned and wheeled me towards the yard and I couldn't stop him. I was shouting at him the whole way that I didn't want to go there and what made him think he had the right to kidnap me.

"You need to see her," he kept insisting. "She misses you."

When we reached the stables and I caught sight of Celine with her head over the door of her stall I began to cry. It was so horrible to be reunited with her there like that, knowing that I couldn't be with her as I used to be before.

"Look! You can still stroke her. Take joy in that!" Dorian encouraged me as Celine stretched her long neck out to me over the stable door. I stroked her muzzle and smelt the warm sweetness of her scent, but it only made me cry harder.

"I want to ride," I sobbed. "And I'm never going to. Don't you see? It's like showing me a feast and telling me I can't eat."

Dorian refused to be defeated by my misery. "You can

still paint her. I've brought your things, you can work from your chair."

He dried my eyes with his handkerchief, held my chin in his hand and raised my face, tilting it so that I was forced to look at him. "Paint me a picture, little sister. Come on. Do it for me, Rose."

There were tears in his eyes, and I realised in all my life I had never seen Dorian cry before. I didn't want him to pity me.

"All right," I sighed. "Set up the easel."

Dorian hurried about before I could change my mind. He swung open the stable door and wheeled me in to sit beside Celine and then set up the easel and adjusted its height while I organised the palette of paints and brushes on my lap. Celine struck a perfect pose with her ears pricked and I settled down and began to work.

And I tried, I really did. But the work did not sing to me. I slapped the paint on and the technique was there at my fingertips as it had always been, but when I drew back and looked, the canvas was mundane and soulless. When I had finished, all I had to show for my three hours in the stables was a portrait of the horse in front of me that had proportion and veracity but absolutely no energy or depth. The beating heart of something deeper that had always been the power of my work, it simply wasn't there.

Dorian couldn't see what was so wrong with it – or at least he pretended he couldn't see it. "It is good for a first attempt after all this time," he insisted as he wheeled me home. "What you need to do is go back to the Paris School, finish the year studying under Demarchelier, and then you can return to your studio and begin to paint again like you used to do. Your gift will return to you. You'll see."

My brother was being kind, but he knew as well as I that this is not how a 'gift' works. Before, when I painted, my portraits expressed the power of nature. Is it because my own nature is so weakened now that my work is limp and bleak? And as for returning to the Paris School. What was the point of that? This was what I tried to explain to Papa tonight at dinner.

"Dorian says you are painting again, so you are ready to return," he said.

"I won't go," I argued. "You can't make me."

"I can," Papa said. "And I will. I am not having you stay at home in a sulk for the rest of your life, Rose. You are going back to school."

A sulk! I am paralysed from the waist down and will

never walk again! I have never liked my father, but today that changed. Now, I hate him. And Dorian too, for being a traitor.

*December 10, 1852*

This morning, when I woke, I knew that I wouldn't get up from my bed. They couldn't make me do it any more. Every day I'd tried. I'd put on a brave face and gone out into the world just to please them: Dorian, Madame Gris, my papa. God, but they are patronising! "Oh, good girl, Rose!" "You are doing so well, Rose!"

Do they think I'm an idiot? What am I doing, exactly, other than trying to please them by pretending to want to be alive? I have nothing left in me. I'm dying here in this claustrophobic room, and yet I can't bear to go outside either. Paris in the springtime is hateful; it glares a cold, hard light on my frailties. I see the way people look at me! The *poor girl*, so sad in her wheelchair.

At art school, Master Demarchelier has taken to fussing over me in an unseemly manner. The other day in class I drew a horse that was so badly proportioned that a child of five could have done better, but he didn't chastise me and point out my failings as an artist. Instead, he was positively rapturous about how beautiful it was. "Well done, Rose!" he said enthusiastically. "I love the use of light and colour! Very good indeed!" And I swivelled my chair wheels around to face him and snapped. "It's not my brain that is damaged. It's just my legs that are useless. I know this work is no good, so don't try and humour me. It's worse than when you hated me."

I tried to storm out of the class after that, but it's not possible in a wheelchair and I got stuck. My wheels wouldn't budge and the master tried to help me to get them free and I swiped at him with my fist, and then I sobbed and sobbed until he got one of the other pupils to fetch my father to come and take me home.


*December 21, 1852*

Papa asked me what I wanted for Christmas and I said, "To walk again." When he sighed a deep sigh and repeated the question, I said, "I want to be left alone, and I want you to stop making me go to school."

So I got my wish. Papa withdrew me from the Paris School and now he no longer makes me do anything I don't want to do. We're having Christmas at Fontainebleau this year. We leave tomorrow, me and Papa, Dorian and

Philippe and Philippe's new wife, Claudette. Also, Papa's sister, Marianne, is coming from Saintes-Maries-de-la-Mer to stay with us. Marianne is Papa's older sister. I haven't seen her for a long time now, but I seem to recall that I like her. I'm not looking forward to Christmas. It will be the first time I've been back to Fontainebleau since the accident.

## December 28, 1852: Fontainebleau

Aunty Marianne is not like a normal aunt. She is very much like myself. She wears trousers instead of skirts, and she likes to smoke little cigars after dinner and she has a laugh that is as hearty as a farmhand's. She tells me not to call her Marianne. "I cannot stand it. It's like an old woman's name." So I call her Mimi, which is the childhood nickname my papa had given her.

When my papa's parents died, the Bonifait family estate was split two ways. Papa got the Paris house and Fontainebleau and Aunty Mimi got Flamants Roses, their large country estate in the Camargue. She lives there now with her friend Chantal. Chantal had to stay on the estate and didn't come with her to Fontainebleau because it's the wet season right now and the rice plantation needs to be sown. Flamants Roses is a very large farm in the marshlands on the coast. It sounds magical. Aunty Mimi breeds bulls there – big black ones – as well as running the rice plantation. The bulls are used for bull-fighting. I admit I got really angry when she told me this.

"They should not be made to fight," I told her over Christmas dinner. "It's barbaric." I had already made a fuss that morning because the Christmas lunch was not vegetarian, so my views hardly seemed surprising to Mimi.

"They do not fight like the bulls in Spain," Mimi insisted. "It's not a blood sport. These bulls have long and happy lives and are very well cared for. I treat them like my own children."

"You don't have your own children," my papa pointed out.

"Because, as I just said, the bulls are my children," Mimi replied snippily.

"I still think it is wrong to make animals do your fighting," I said.

"Would you come and visit me and see my bulls, Rose?" Mimi smiled. "And my horses of course."

"You breed horses too?" Dorian asked.

"Not exactly," Mimi said. "They are wild, the horses of the Camargue. They roam our lands at will. Once or twice a year the gardians, who are the cowboys, the gauchos who manage my land, they herd them all together and they brand them and care for the young ones, break the older ones in under saddle so that they can be ridden. Then they let them loose again in winter and they run wild and free in the sea."

"In the sea?" I became interested in spite of myself.

"Yes," Mimi said. "The Camargue is a tidal swamp, and the horses are accustomed to having wet feet. They graze on the sea grass and they run through the waves and they are all coloured grey like the skies and the oceans – they are very beautiful."

She smiled at me again. "So you'll come and stay? Your father says you have no more school. We have plenty of room. It would be fun, I promise."

It strikes me now that this is what Mimi and my papa had planned all along. Tonight, I was just making my way to bed when I heard voices in the study. I wheeled my chair up the hall and through a crack in the door I could see them in there – Papa and Mimi – both of them sitting in enormous leather armchairs at the edge of the fireplace. The fire was crackling very loudly as the wood split and bubbled in the grate. My papa and Mimi were both smoking cigars and enjoying some dark reddish-brown liquid in crystal glasses, and they were talking in very serious voices. The topic of the conversation was me.

"I hope you are aware of what you are taking on," Papa was saying. "Rose has never been an easy child to raise. She's always been wilful, and refused to do things in a way that most girls do. Now, since her accident, it has become impossible to reason with her."

Aunty Mimi's voice was gravelly but warm. "Being obstinate and headstrong are good qualities in a girl as far as I'm concerned. I was the same as a child, wasn't I?"

"Yes. And look how you turned out!" Papa growled.

Through the gap in the door I saw Mimi reach out and clasp my papa's hand, and I must say I was shocked to see that a genuine affection existed between sister and brother – just as it is with Dorian and me.

"Jacques, listen to me. You know what I am saying makes sense. Rose will go mad if you continue to coop her up in that apartment. The life you had planned for her, the Parisian artist, it ceased to exist on the day that pheasant flew up from beneath her horse's hooves. I am offering her a new future. Take the opportunity with both hands, Jacques, because you know if you do not let Rose come with me, her resentment, the pain of losing her liberty, it will be turned back on you. Or worse still, on herself."

My papa went quiet and then he said. "I cannot bear to look at her, Marianne. My own child and I cannot turn my eyes on her . . ."

And at the moment my wheelchair rolled forward slightly and I heard the floorboards beneath the wheels give a very loud creak.

I was worried that Papa and Mimi would hear it too, but they must have thought it was just the crackling of the wood in the fireplace because they carried on talking. And I left and continued to my room.

Now, I lie here in the darkness, and I think about what I have been reduced to. My own father admits it! He cannot stand the sight of me now that I am a cripple. I am being sent away to the salt marshes where he no longer has to confront what I have become. Well, that is fine by me. Whatever lies ahead of me, it cannot be worse than this.

CHAPTER 9

## *Terror at the Louvre*

Rose had resigned herself to leave Paris, but I felt I couldn't quit now – even though each day Augustin confirmed his lack of faith in my talent. In the weeks that followed, I did all that I could to work on my art – I went to the Célestins almost every day, spending hours drawing Claude. Despite what Augustin believed, I was trying. I listened in class to everything he said and I took it on board. I was improving too. My sketches now had a flow, a gracefulness of line that I hadn't possessed before. I could see myself maturing as an artist – even if Augustin could not.

"You have developed even greater technique," he said grudgingly as we sat down for my half-term assessment. "But you still lack emotion. Where is your heart, Maisie?

Why won't you let it show? And the work, it is just not contemporary. Look at what everyone else in the class is producing around you! Modern art should be thought-provoking and say something about the world we live in today. And you bring me portrait after portrait of horses . . ." Augustin carried on telling me how awful my art was and then he delivered the final blow. "It is not good enough, I am afraid. I will not put this work forward for the auction intake. My professional reputation as an educator is at stake here. You need to bring me something else before the end of term or you will not earn a place in the selection of work to be sold at Lucie's."

All term I'd been trying to convince myself that I didn't care what Augustin said. I was following in the footsteps of Rose Bonifait – and if she could stick to her guns, then I could too. But his words that day rocked me.

"But can he really do that?" Oscar asked when I arrived at the Célestins and told him what had just happened. "Surely you have had your fees paid and your work should be sold at the student auction?"

"Being included in the auction is reserved for the very best pupils," I said. "Augustin is the decider. I can't make him include me."

Claude, who had been standing over in the corner of the stall as we spoke, came over to us now and stuck his head over the loose box door. I gave his velvet muzzle a stroke and saw the worry in his eyes.

"It's not your fault, Claude," I told him firmly. "You're a good model. It's me that Augustin doesn't like."

"What's he talking about anyway?" Oscar continued. "This auction he refers to?"

"It's a tradition at the school," I said. "The pupils all produce a work and the top achievers have their art sold under the hammer at Lucie's."

"Lucie's?" Oscar said. "Really?"

"You know it?"

"It's a very famous auction house," Oscar said. "So famous that even I have heard of it. Lucie's is very grand. All the bourgeoisie go there to buy fancy things for enormous prices."

"What's a bourgeoisie?"

"Somebody who is rich and pretentious," Oscar said. "I think in English you might call them social climbers? Trying to impress each other with their money and fancy things. You know the kind."

"No," I said. "I don't."

I didn't know any rich people back home. I certainly

didn't have an insight into what kind of art they liked, but I was pretty sure it would be all the modern stuff that Augustin was trying to make me do. I didn't think they would go wild in a bidding war over a portrait of a police horse.

Augustin had decided it wasn't enough to just tell me that I wasn't good enough to be in the auction. He'd told Madame Richard, as well. And, of course, she had told Nicole.

"Madame Richard says Augustin is very concerned about you," Nicole explained over dinner.

I pushed my food around on my plate, not sure how to respond. "Augustin isn't concerned," I said. "He just hates my work."

"Maisie," Nicole said gently. "I'm sure that's not true."

"It is!" I shoved my plate away. I'd lost my appetite. I felt sick. "He told me again today that my art still isn't good enough."

"That's just ridiculous," Françoise almost choked on her food as she leapt to my defence. "I love your pictures of Claude!"

"Well, Augustin doesn't love them," I said. "He likes art that is modern."

Françoise huffed at this. "So you are supposed to just become a clone and do whatever Augustin likes? I thought art was about having your own ideas? What is original about doing what everyone else in the class is doing?"

Nicole frowned. "Françoise has a point. You must be true to yourself, Maisie. Good art can never be made by pretending to be someone else."

Nicole put her hands to her throat and fiddled with a large gold necklace that she often wore that was studded with tourmaline and tiger's eye. "All the same, Augustin is a great teacher, his opinion is very respected. For him, I know, there is much at stake with the Lucie's auction looming. The cream of Paris society will be out in force to snap up the work of his students, and the success of this society event is all riding on Augustin. He is the gatekeeper, choosing which work is good enough to put forward for auction. He is incorruptible too. He will never hand over anything that does not genuinely meet his exacting standards. To do so would be to destroy the esteemed name of the Paris School itself."

Nicole placed both her palms flat on the table decisively. "Maisie, we need to solve this problem. I can see now I have not done enough since you arrived in Paris to expand your vision and feed your creative spirit. You are young, and it is only natural that you lack the historical perspective the older pupils in your class possess. To develop your art in the contemporary way Augustin wishes you to do, you should be exposed to the galleries here where all the best examples of those kinds of work are held. Tomorrow, Françoise will take you to the Pompidou Centre and the Louvre. The famous artists you see hung on the walls there may inspire you to progress in your own art."

"The Pompidou and the Louvre?" Françoise groaned. "Maman! There will be queues of tourists for miles!"

"Do you want to help Maisie or not?" Nicole replied. "Then get out the door by nine and you two will be at the front of the queue before anyone else has had their morning coffee!"

\*\*\*

"Maisie! Wake up, we are late already!" Françoise was at my door the next morning at nine, yawning and still in her pyjamas. We dressed in haste to make up lost time but by the time we'd had croissants and hot chocolate it was almost ten. We walked briskly through the streets towards the Pompidou Centre. "Come on!" Françoise kept coaxing me to go faster. "The crowds, oh the crowds!"

The Pompidou already had a queue when we arrived. The building looked like a spaceship – covered with weird plastic test tubes housing the escalators to the different levels.

As we swept from floor to floor, I tried hard to take it all in as Françoise led the charge through art eras from the surrealists, to cubists and postmodernists.

In the Dadaist wing, Françoise pointed out the painting of the Mona Lisa with a moustache drawn on her. "That is Duchamp. And that is too, and that one," she pointed at a urinal sitting in the middle of the room.

"Is that a toilet?" I said.

"No." Françoise looked at me like I was stupid. "It's art."

"This is why Augustin and I are never ever going to understand each other," I grumbled to Françoise.

"This is too modern for you, I think." Françoise shrugged. "You'll like the Louvre better. It's full of the old stuff."

To get inside the Louvre you had to enter through a big glass pyramid. Once we were inside we had to queue for an hour to see the real *Mona Lisa* – which looked just like the one at the Pompidou with the moustache only now there was no moustache, so that was a waste of time.

From there, we roamed each and every room, and I found myself awash in a sea of antiquity; cherubs flying and angels playing harps and statues of naked women with no arms. It was all beautiful, and I could see how amazingly clever the artists must have been to paint them or carve them out of marble, you know, all of that, but even though I could see the works were important, none of them truly connected with me. Until I came into a room of nineteenth-century art. Here, one wall of the room was taken up by a massive painting, almost half the length of the gallery wall. The painting drew me to it and I stood in front of it and felt dwarfed by its size and power.

It was a painting of horses. There were almost a dozen of them in the image, a wild herd, all of them grey. In the foreground there was a cluster of mares, some with young foals at foot, and behind them were the stallions standing guard over the rest, gazing imperiously to the horizon where the coastline was battered by the wild, roiling grey-blue waves of the ocean. This was a desolate and remote landscape where the surf was rough, the skies were darkened and stormy and the tempestuous weather was clearly maddening for the horses. Some of them were fighting against the wild weather, shaking their heads and flinging their manes. Two young colts to the far left of the frame were engaged in a fight, rearing up on their hinds legs, although it looked like their battle was nothing more than play to let off a little steam.

The real focus of the artwork, though, was at the centre of the painting. A proud and stoic grey mare, who weathered the storm that was raging about her and focused her gaze on the young colt that was at her flank. He looked so newborn that his legs could barely hold him up. He was vulnerable and precious, as if all the things that were pure and good in the world belonged in that one moment just to him. And the painting itself – it was remarkable. It was both real and magical at the same time. The technique was so flawless it could almost have been a photograph, and yet at the same time there was so much of the artist's heart and soul on display. It moved me in a way no art, not even the mighty *Whistlejacket*, had ever done before.

I was so consumed by it, the crowds of tourists around me melted away and I was awash in the grey seas that expanded before me. How did the artist make each and every brush stroke so perfect, how did they give the horses such depth and character? This painting in front of me now was exactly what I wanted to do with my own work, to capture the very essence of nature armed with nothing more than oils and brushes. I didn't care what Augustin said about art being modern. I wanted to paint something *real* and to have it be as good as this art that hung before me now. Finally, I tore my eyes away from the work itself and I stepped forward at last so that I could read the plaque beneath:

Rose Bonifait, *Grignons de Camargue*, 1853.

***

"She has this way of doing their tails, so that the colours of the hairs are all very different, taupe and mustard, charcoal and white but together they mingle into grey and it looks so lifelike . . ." I raved on to Françoise as we walked back upstairs heading up and into the glass pyramid space so that we could exit through the gift shop to leave the Louvre.

I had not stopped talking about Rose since I saw the painting. I was still processing its significance, I think. It was an amazing work, and what made it even more amazing for me was the date on it – 1853. So Rose had painted it after she became paralysed.

Françoise, though, was barely listening to me. She was whingeing about the Louvre again. "The crush of people to get out is even worse than it was to get in!" she complained as we pushed through the doors.

"It's not just the crowds," I said. "There's something else going on outside."

We were trying to leave, but for some reason everyone else was pushing past us in the opposite direction, back inside the museum.

"Get inside!" Somebody shouted at us. "Get inside now!"

Suddenly the mad surge of people coming at us was no longer just a crowd of annoying tourists. They were a panic-stricken mob! There were people with terror in their eyes, fighting to get in – running and shoving, all of them desperate to get inside the building. We were stuck in the crowd and I was calling out to Françoise.

I'd lost her completely and then I felt her hand grasp mine and pull me forward and suddenly the both of us were out on the street and there were more people, pushing us, shoving us.

"Françoise?" I felt panic rising in me now too. "Françoise? What's going on?"

And then there was the deafening sound of police sirens wailing through the air, and a *pop-pop-pop* like fireworks and smoke fizzing up from the cobblestones. Smoke bombs, thrown by the police, had landed on the ground outside the pyramid. They let out long silver plumes of smoke shrouding the square around the Louvre.

All around us now, people were no longer just pushing and shouting. Now they began to scream. I was still blocking the Louvre exit and one man pushed past me so hard that I fell over. Françoise helped me back to my feet again.

"Come on!" she said. "We need to get out of here."

I ran after her, panting, terrified. The smoke from the bombs was making my eyes stream and it was hard to see where I was going.

And then, across the road, on the other side of the square, I saw Oscar and Claude.

Oscar wore a high-vis vest, and he rode alongside three other mounted officers on chestnut horses. They were blowing whistles, signalling and moving the crowds along, beckoning for people to move out of the open street and into the buildings that bordered the square.

"That's Claude!" I pointed him out to Françoise. "The horse? The one from my pictures? It's him –"

I didn't get to finish because over the sound of the sirens and the bombs, suddenly another noise cut through. There was a car, the engine revving, tyres squealing and more screams now, people yelling and crying out.

Across the courtyard, people were scattering, running in every direction as the car – well, it was a van, I could see it now, a white van – going as fast as if it were on a motorway, sped right through the crowds.

"What's he doing?" Françoise said. "Hey! He can't drive through here, it's pedestrians only!"

And that was when I realised what the van was doing. "He's going to hit the pyramid!" I said. "He's doing it on purpose! Françoise, we need to run!"

By then, though, the crowds were pushing us back towards the Louvre, but I fought my way out, heading towards Claude and Oscar.

"This way!" I called to Françoise. "Run!"

I began to sprint across the square as the van mounted the kerb, still driving straight for the pyramid.

"Françoise . . ." I had thought she'd been running right behind me, but she must have been swept up in the crowd and forced back towards the Louvre entrance. I could see her now, far behind me and only just now breaking free of the crush, running to catch me.

"Françoise!"

I screamed as the van veered towards her. There were police cars chasing it, driving fast through the smoke haze and the siren noise. And at the same time I saw Oscar and Claude heading towards the pyramid too, galloping over the cobbles at breakneck speed. At first I thought their intention was to get to Françoise before the van could strike, so that Oscar could scoop her up on to Claude's back with him and out of harm's way, the way a knight swoops and picks up a princess. But this was not a fairy story, this was a horror story, and such a move now was impossible. Instead, Oscar, as a trained policeman, had seen Françoise in the path of the van and had immediately understood that he must commit to an action that had only one outcome.

What happened next would have a hundred witnesses.

The people directly inside the pyramid had a ringside seat to it all. As the van bore down on the pyramid they realised they had nowhere to escape and all they could do was watch it come for them. Except . . . then the young gendarme of the Garde républicaine came riding on his enormous black horse, galloping hard, coming straight at the pyramid from the opposite direction so that at the very last moment he appeared to confront the van. And before anyone could really understand what had just happened, there was the most sickening screech of tyres and the smell of rubber and then the horrible thud of flesh on metal as Oscar and Claude took the full impact and the van ploughed straight into both of them.

Claude's legs buckled as he went down and then he and Oscar both disappeared. And then before I could even gasp for breath, the noise was deafening as the crowd broke free of the Louvre pyramid, and all of a sudden the courtyard was in the grip of mass panic. People were running at me! Trying to get as far as they could from the van and the pyramid, and within seconds I was being thrown to the ground and trampled and trapped by the crush of bodies above me. I felt myself being kicked in the head as I tried to stand and I was certain I would be killed, and then suddenly I felt a hand reach out to me.

"Maisie!" Françoise dragged me back to my feet. "Come on! We have to get out of here!"

I was shaking with shock and horror, but she had her arm around me. "Run, Maisie!" And although my mind was reeling my body obeyed and we did the only thing we could. We ran.

CHAPTER 10

## *Flamants Roses*

Sixteen missed calls blinked up in neon green on Françoise's phone – all of them were from Nicole.

"It is all over the news!" Nicole told Françoise when she called back. "Are you safe? Tell me where you are! I'll come for you."

We sheltered in the doorway of a fancy boutique on the rue de Rivoli and minutes later Nicole arrived. When she leapt out of the car and clutched Françoise to her, the tears in her eyes made me suddenly miss my dad, and I realised the news of what had happened had probably gone global already.

"I should call him in case he's worried about me," I told Nicole.

She gave me her phone – mine had been lost in the rush. "Of course. Let him know you are OK."

There was such relief in my dad's voice when he heard me over the phone. He'd been trying to call me too. "It's all over the BBC," he said. "They're calling it a terror attack."

He hadn't realised, of course, just how close I had been at the time and when I told him I was actually at the Louvre when it happened – well, that was a big mistake!

"Maisie, I want you on the next flight out of there," he said.

"Dad, that's ridiculous!" I said. "I'm fine. I don't want to come home."

"Maisie . . ."

"Dad, please . . ."

All the way home in the car we fought about it. I could see why my dad was so worried, but like I said to him, terror attacks happen in London too! What surprised me when I was talking to him was how much I wanted to stay in Paris. Even though things had been tough at art school, it seemed like the wrong thing to leave now. What was keeping me here the most was Claude and Oscar. Reports on the attack were coming through non-stop on the news. They said the horse and the gendarme were both alive but in a serious condition. I kept thinking there must have been a way I could have helped them, somehow gone back to them after the van had struck. At the time, though, we'd been running for our lives, and after that . . .?

"You would never have got through the police cordon," Nicole said. Which was probably true, but now it was all over, I knew I needed to see them. Except I didn't know where to begin to find them.

"Leave that to me," Nicole said. She made some calls, and by the time we were home again, Nicole's team had tracked Oscar down to the local hospital on the Île de la Cité.

"They tell me he is stable, which is good news, but they have him in intensive care and he isn't allowed visitors yet," Nicole said.

"What about Claude?" I asked.

"Claude is back at the Célestins stables and the vets are with him now."

"Is he going to be OK?" I felt my heart race. I had seen the way the van had struck him down. Claude had been right in the path of the vehicle. I kept seeing him in that moment when he charged forward at a gallop, the terror in his eyes and that look on Oscar's face too as he realised what they both had to do. There had not been a split second of hesitation from either of them – they were there to protect the public and they did their job. And now . . . who knew? I felt sick with worry for them both.

"They won't say anything about what is wrong, but they admit that Claude is critical," Nicole continued. "Leave the vets to do their work, Maisie. I promise you, if there's no more news by morning, we'll go down there and force our way in to see him if we have to, OK?"

So I went to my room and pulled out my sketch book and looked at my drawings of Claude. Oh, but he was such a handsome horse! And then as I flicked through the stack, my eyes took on a fresh perspective, and for the first time I could see the truth – there was something missing in my pictures. I had this sickening feeling as I scanned the sketches. Augustin had been right all along about my work. I was holding something back in my heart, not truly expressing myself. These old drawings that he had so disliked, I could see their fatal flaw now too. They lacked emotion; they had no soul.

I curled up on my bed, still shaking a little from the

day's events. I looked at the clock. It was still only 4 p.m.! How could the world have changed so much, so fast? My mind was racing, and in an effort to drown out the fear that haunted me, I turned to Rose's diary once more. I opened the page to where I had left it last time and began to read.

*February 10, 1853*

I have been cooped up for eight days in the carriage journeying to Saintes-Maries-de-la-Mer. Eight days with nothing to do! Yes, I tried to draw. But the roads were too bumpy, and I couldn't keep the pencil steady. And I tried to read a book, but I felt sick, so instead I just stared out of the windows at the countryside. France, it turns out, is full of trees.

We overnighted in small inns along the route in Nevers, Moulins, Le Puy and Avignon. Each evening upon arrival the coachman would uncouple the horses and feed them and put them in the stalls below the inn with hay and water. Such lovely horses – a team of four – all of them dark bay. There was a time when I would have helped the coachman to tend and groom them. Now I couldn't even tend to myself. I needed help to get anywhere at the inns as there were too many stairs to use my wheelchair so it got left on board the coach. I hate that chair anyway. It is so slow and cumbersome! It cannot cope with rutted ground or grassy terrain. It is a useless thing.

But then I am a useless thing too. I can't move without the chair. So we are two useless things together.

It was midday when I arrived at Flamants Roses. There was a sign at the gate, but all the same, once we drove up to the house I was in disbelief.

"Is this it?" I asked the coachman. "Really?"

The house was a simple square stone building with a grey slate roof. The stone must have been painted a pale pink at some point, but so much of it was now lost beneath the overgrowth of rambling roses that smothered the façade, it was hard to tell.

The gardens, too, were overgrown as if nobody lived here, and beyond them the rest of the farm seemed like nothing more than a few outlying sheds bordered by swamp waters. I was underwhelmed. I had expected a mansion to rival the grandeur of our family chateau in Fontainebleau. Aunt Mimi seemed to have got the short straw when it came to inheritance. So this was to be my new home?

Even more distressing, after a whole week of travel to get here, there was nobody waiting to greet me. I sat in my wheelchair, wondering what to do, when suddenly I heard the barking of dogs. A moment later, two enormous beasts came bounding around the southern end of the house. They were strapping great dogs. Hunting hounds I guessed by their sleek physique, but not like any I had seen before. They had black heads and their bodies were speckled like a plover's egg. Their long, floppy ears swept behind them and bright pink tongues lolled from their mouths as they ran to me. In just a few strides they were upon me and I was in danger of being licked to death as they smothered me with kisses. A moment later, a dark-haired woman in a very modern white-and-blue striped dress, that had none of the usual Parisian fancies like a tight bodice and a crinoline hoop, came striding around the house from the same direction. She was very pretty even in her plain gown, and she had a bright smile on her face as she called to them. "Berlioz, Balzac!! Heel!"

The two dogs whimpered as if they were children who had been caught being particularly naughty and they went straight to her, tails wagging. They fell into step at her side as she approached me.

"It is so lovely to meet you, Mimi has been so excited about your arrival!" Chantal greeted me warmly. She took the handles of my chair and began to wheel me to the house, chatting away as if we were already great friends. "She is out bringing in the bulls with the gardians," she said. "I packed us a lunch to take to her. We'll put your bags inside and then depart. Now, where is Pierre to get your bags? Pierre!"

We had come around the back of the house, and here the swampy fields became a lake. There were two small punting boats moored up next to a tiny jetty, and in one of those boats a boy about my age was lazing with his hat tilted down over his face to keep the sun off. At the sound of Chantal calling his name, he roused himself dozily out of the vessel, tilted the hat back and sat up.

"All set to go!" he said, trying to act as if he hadn't just been fast asleep.

"Then grab Rose's bags and take them inside and we'll be off," Chantal said. "The gardians will be waiting for their lunch."

Pierre got up lazily, and there was something about the way he walked towards me that made me feel as if he were more accustomed to being on the water than land.

I liked him straight away. He had sandy blond hair, and freckles on his tanned cheeks, and his eyes smiled even more readily than his mouth. He reminded me a little of Dorian.

He went and took my bags indoors and meanwhile Chantal loaded wicker baskets into the front of one of the boats.

"You can take Rose in your boat," Chantal told Pierre when he returned.

Pierre stared at me. "How do I get her into the boat?"

Chantal rolled her eyes. "Lift her, of course!"

And he did. This totally strange lad I'd never met before stood in front of my wheelchair and lifted me up and plonked me down on the prow bench of the punting boat as if I were a sack of flour being taken to market.

"Hey!" I squeaked.

It was such a different motion – bobbing up and down inside a tiny boat after a week inside a cramped horse carriage. I looked over the edge into the water and saw that it was shallow and murky beneath us.

"When the tide is out, the boat may sometimes touch the bottom with two of us in it," Pierre said, clearly not realising that my objection was to being thrown into a boat rather than whether the water was deep enough. "This is high tide now, though, so we will float, I'm sure."

And with me in the prow, and Chantal accompanying us in the boat alongside – which was stacked high at one end with wicker baskets – Pierre used a stick to punt us off from the shore. Then he stood up and used it to strike the bottom of the swamp and push us on. Chantal did the same thing in her vessel.

"Why don't you just row?" I asked.

"The water isn't deep enough to scoop in the oars," Pierre said poking the punting pole down to show me just how shallow it was. "Punting is easier, especially as we get further into the rice paddies."

On the carriage ride from Paris we had passed many wheat fields, and these rice paddies looked a little like them, except that instead of being planted in the ground, these crops were in water, with tiny canals that we could punt along between the rows. We moved silently through the rice fields, sometimes scaring a duck here and there off its nest so that it would quack accusations at us as we glided gently past. Beyond the paddies, we entered the estuaries where the groomed landscape gave way to the wilderness of the salt marshes. Here, the only things that grew in this bitter, salty soil were stalky outcrops of sea lavender and grey-green purslane. Wading through the expanses of these slowly moving waterways was a flock of pink flamingos. They had such long legs that the water only came up to their knee joints. Their plumage was unlike that of any bird I had ever seen, with feathers the colour of a rose-tinted sunset.

"It's from the pink flamingos that Flamants Roses takes its name," Chantal told me as she manoeuvred through the flock, and we punted behind her. I marvelled at the casual ease with which she handled the boat, leaning right over on the wooden pole to drag herself this way and that. We were winding our way through the waters, and up ahead I could see an island of sorts, an expanse of firm, dry land heavy with scrubby undergrowth. We beached on the shore of the island and Chantal pulled her boat up on to the sand so it wouldn't float away and then Pierre did the same with me still on board.

"Wait here," he said to me without any irony.

"What else would I do?" I replied.

They walked off together into the scrub and the trees and left me there! And what followed seemed like the longest wait of my life – and remember I had just been in a carriage for eight straight days. I listened to the cries of the birds, felt the heat of the sun burning the back of my neck, wished I had worn a hat and was glad I was in trousers at least to keep the mosquitoes at bay as they were buzzing around me like tiny demons.

Chantal and Pierre had disappeared completely from view, I should add. They had walked into the trees directly ahead of me and now they were nowhere to be seen. And so I waited. And just when I was about to begin to shout out for help, fearing I had been abandoned, I heard the thunder of hoof beats.

Through the trees the sounds echoed, hoof beats and voices crying out. And then from the forest before me, the bulls burst forth. There were three of them. Enormous black creatures. They charged out of the undergrowth with the whites of their eyes showing, their horns glinting in the sun. Even if I hadn't been a regular at the abattoir, there was no mistaking these creatures in front of me for cows. Only bulls looked like this, with long horns, broad brows and massive necks set into powerful shoulders. These were creatures whose whole being was built for fighting. And now they were thundering out of the forest, and all that lay between them and the sea was me – sitting there helplessly in my shallow-bottomed boat.

I would have screamed at that moment – I admit it. I was terrified. Luckily, I didn't have the chance to make a fool of myself because before I could shriek or squeal, the gardians emerged behind the bulls. There were three of them too, mounted on great grey horses. The gardian who rode at the head of the three charged directly towards me, outstripping the bulls for speed, and then he turned his grey horse so that the sand skidded up from beneath his hooves. Reaching down, he plucked me out of my boat and threw me up behind him so that I sat across the horse's flanks directly behind the saddle.

"Hold tight around my waist!" he instructed.

And he turned his horse on its hocks and rode out of the way of the bulls while, at the same time, the two remaining gardians used their capes and sticks to lure and herd the bulls away from us. At one point, the bulls actually ran into the sea. Even then, the horses continued to give chase, cantering as they hit the water, splashing noisily as they followed after the bulls who were now knee-deep in the waves ahead of them.

"These three bulls, they are trouble," the gardian said to me over his shoulder. "They constantly run wild through the rice paddies and ruin the crops. Today it has taken all three of us to hunt them out of the forest so that we can take them home and reunite them with the herd. I tell the Maitresse that we should give them up to the matadors to be used for sport. They are bad bulls! We would be better off without them. But she will not listen. She is stubborn! She is impossible –"

"She is right behind you!"

Out of the forest now emerged a woman on yet another grey horse, almost identical to the ones ridden by the gardians.

"Antoine, we are not giving up my bulls to those brutes just because they misbehave from time to time. All God's creatures deserve a happy life, even you!" my aunty Mimi barked in a good-natured fashion at her embarrassed gardian. Then, flanked on either side by Chantal and Pierre, also on grey horses identical to the rest, she rode towards me. I noticed how she rode with her legs long in the stirrups like the gardians did, and with her reins in one hand too – so unlike the Parisian style of equitation. Yet it suited her, and she looked so at home on that horse. And in that moment, as she smiled at me in a way that made me realise I was truly welcome in this strange, wild place, I realised I might somehow have found a home too.

"Beloved niece. Welcome to Flamants Roses."

## Chapter 11

# *Death's Dark Spectre*

I was roused from my exhausted sleep later that evening by Nicole. I took one look at her face and knew it was good news.

"Oscar's going to be OK. He's no longer in intensive care. He's awake and he's asking to see you, Maisie."

I was stunned. "Me? But why?"

"I don't know," Nicole admitted. "The hospital gave no more details. So, hurry now, grab your coat. My driver is bringing the car around to the front for us."

We stopped quickly at Ladurée just before the doors closed and I got Oscar a big box of macarons – a rainbow selection, as I didn't want to take the time choosing flavours as we were in a rush.

In the hospital they led me to Oscar's room. He was

sitting up in bed looking pale and dishevelled. His arm was in a cast, and he had stitches above his right eyebrow that zigzagged across his forehead.

"You look like Harry Potter," I blurted out. Oscar gave a laugh and then regretted it, wincing in pain.

"I have cracked ribs," he explained. "It hurts to laugh."

"I'll try not to be funny then," I said.

Apart from the Harry Potter scar, Oscar had a belly scar too, where they had operated to take out his spleen because it had been ruptured when the van struck. His collarbone and his arm were both broken, and the head injury was still worrying the doctors.

"I have a small brain bleed." Oscar shrugged. "They are doing scans and they might need to operate again – but on here this time." He rapped with his knuckles on his skull.

"They'll cut your head open?" I was horrified.

"It's not so bad, they say," Oscar said. "But it will be a while before I can leave, and I am worried about Claude."

"Is he OK?" I asked.

"He is back at the Célestins, but his injuries are bad. Alexandre says they nearly put him down on the spot but he begged them to at least take him back to the stables and let the vet take a look at him." Oscar's eyes filled with tears. "He is a good horse . . . well, I don't have to tell you this. You know how amazing and gentle he is, but he has such a dislike of vets. Ever since he was a young colt he's been very scared of them, and he hates injections, needles, that kind of thing. He'll be hard to treat because of this, and I worry that they will give up on him. I need someone there with him, someone to reassure him and calm him."

"Alexandre is there though, isn't he?"

"Not all the time." Oscar shook his head. "He is on duty. And there is no one else in the yard that Claude trusts. I've seen how much he likes you. Right from the start when you first came to draw him and sit in his stall, I could see that he had a bond with you. He needs that now. He needs a friend. Maisie, I know it is a lot to ask . . ."

"No," I said. "I mean, no, it's not a lot to ask. I want to help Claude. Of course I'll go and be with him."

I didn't tell Oscar about Augustin and the threats he'd made to me about not being able to take part in the looming art auction if I didn't deliver anything worthy. If Oscar had known I only had a couple of weeks left to produce an artwork that would finally please my teacher, well, he was so kind he would have told me to go home instead and focus on my art. But I didn't even care about the Paris School at that moment, and the truth was that even if Oscar hadn't asked me to be with him, nothing would have kept me from Claude's side.

"They will be waiting for you at the Célestins," Oscar said. "I have told Alexandre you are coming tonight. He will meet you at the gate."

Nicole's driver took me there. It was raining by then, and night had fallen as we drove through the same Paris streets that had been bathed in pink light only that morning. Now the city felt entirely different to me. The rain made it look as if Paris was weeping, the streets turned blue and grey, except for the pools of white street lights and the raindrops dazzling like diamonds as they fell.

Alexandre stood at the gates waiting for me in the rain, the peak of his Garde républicaine hat all that was visible of his face beneath the black cloak of his raincoat. I leapt out of the car and ran across the wet cobblestones to him.

"How is he doing?" I asked.

"You are in time. He is still alive," Alexandre said.

The reply shocked me to my core. I hadn't realised until he said these words that it was possible Claude might have died before I could even reach his side. I was shocked too when Alexandre gripped my arm tight and held me back, stopping me in my tracks.

"I need to prepare you, Maisie, for what you are about to see. His injuries, they are very serious indeed. I haven't really told Oscar how bad his wounds are as I didn't want him to get upset."

I could feel myself shaking now as I asked the question.

"Is he going to die?"

"It is hard to know. The vet came to assess the extent of his injuries but he couldn't get a needle in to sedate him. Claude fought violently every time he tried to get close to him."

Alexandre was still holding my arm. He looked at me very hard and serious now. "Promise me, Maisie, when you are in his stall you will keep your wits about you. Claude is not the horse that you knew. In this condition right now he is dangerous. There is talk from the head of the Célestins that he may still have to be put down."

"Oscar would never allow that!" I was horrified.

"Oscar has no say in such matters," Alexandre said. "Claude is not his horse, he belongs to the Célestins. If his wounds are too extreme, what else is there for it?"

So I understood now how grave the situation was as we hurried side by side through the courtyard in the rain. Up ahead in the corridor I could see Claude's loose box with the lights on inside.

"He's alone in there. The vet is coming back again soon," Alexandre said. "In the meantime, perhaps if you sit with him? But please, Maisie, be careful. I tried to approach him earlier and . . ."

Alexandre pushed back the long sleeve of his raincoat and I saw that underneath his shirt was ripped and there was a nasty purple bruise with two livid red marks where Claude had clearly sunk his teeth into his flesh.

"He did that to you?"

"I was trying to check the wound," Alexandre said. "He got angry. It was my fault, I should have tied his head off, but then he gets so furious if he is restrained . . ."

None of this – the attacks, the fear, the fury – sounded like the Claude I knew.

At the door, Alexandre stepped back. "He might react better if it is just you that he sees," he explained.

I unbolted the lower door of the stall and walked inside.

"Claude?"

He was in the furthest corner of the stall, lying prone on the straw. The way his head hung down low so that his muzzle rested over his forelegs on to the floor almost broke my heart straight away, and the sound of his breathing! It was so loud it echoed in the stall, each gasp more laboured and rasping than the last.

As I got closer, I could see that his flanks were heaving and he was drenched in sweat. And the wound on his leg was even more horrific than I had anticipated. It looked like something out of Rose Bonifait's abattoir visits – an open gash that ran almost the full length of his haunches, and near the hock the skin had split away and the flesh had been gouged so that I was pretty certain I could see all the way through muscle and sinew and down to the bone itself. It looked like the leg was broken too, it stuck out at such an impossible angle, and now I was trailing my eyes down it and, yes, there was more blood and swelling all the way down to the fetlock.

135

But if the leg was disturbing to see, what worried me most were the hidden injuries. I'd seen the way the van had struck Claude and knocked him down so that he was crushed beneath the wheels. It was entirely possible that they had run over his body and Claude had internal wounds, too.

I stepped closer, watching his laboured breathing, his glassy eyes. There was a foam of white sweat on his neck and he still hadn't raised his head to look at me.

"Claude?"

When I spoke his name, I had hoped he would hear my voice and respond. But he didn't, he just lay there. I felt my heart choking in my chest at the sight of him. My own breath now came out in little sobs and I was about to burst into tears when I heard the loose box door behind me open again.

A torrent of French words. I looked up and a burly man in navy overalls was standing there holding a syringe with a long needle in the end of it.

"What?" I looked at him blankly. "I can't speak French."

The man disappeared and when he came back, he had Alexandre with him to translate.

"This is Marcel, the vet. He says he wants you to

move away from the horse, that he's dangerous. But I have explained to him who you are."

"What's in the injection?"

"A painkiller and antibiotics to fight infection from the leg wound," Alexandre said.

I looked at Claude on the floor. His ears were flattened in anger, his muzzle wrinkled in fury. He had refused to let Marcel near him last time and this time would be no different.

"Claude trusts me. Maybe if I hold his head the vet can get the injection in?"

The vet looked dubious as Alexandre explained this.

"Claude knows me," I repeated.

Alexandre and the vet both came into the stall now and stood beside me next to Claude.

"OK, if you take his head then . . ." Alexandre began, but Claude knew what was coming and before I could even get near him to take hold of his halter, he began to flail about, teeth bared and his neck whip-lashing like some creature from a Greek myth that had suddenly burst to life. All three of us scrambled back, getting out of the way just in time.

The vet was speaking French again. I had the feeling it was mostly swear words.

I looked at Alexandre. "I can do it by myself."

"What?" Alexandre shook his head in disbelief. "Don't be ridiculous, Maisie."

"Get the vet to direct me. I'll do it."

Alexandre looked sceptical, but I think he knew it was the only way.

He handed me the syringe. I waited for them to leave and shut the bottom door and then I stepped forward and knelt down beside Claude, hiding the syringe on the floor behind me.

"Hey, Claude," I whispered softly to him. "It's me. Oscar sent me to check up on you."

Claude had laid his ears back, flat against his head. But I kept talking, kept saying his name over and over, and then I saw it. One of the ears flicked up and turned to me. He was listening. Then I saw a softening in his eyes and I took my chance. I reached forward and stroked his muzzle. Claude gave a sigh, and the sound was so full of despair it was heart-breaking.

"I'm going to help you, Claude," I whispered to him. "I swear. I won't let them harm you, but you have to let me do something to you, OK? It's just a little scratch, I promise."

"OK." Alexandre was at the door, guiding me in English as the vet gave him instructions in French. "This injection has to be into the muscle. You see on Claude's neck there is an area below the mane? Put your hand on it."

I did as he said.

"Very good," Alexandre said. "That is where the injection needs to go. Take your hand away now. Use the other hand to thrust the needle in. You will have to punch down quite hard, I'm afraid, to get it into the muscle. He may try to bite when you do this."

I took my hand away and surreptitiously picked up the syringe. Talking to Claude the whole time, holding his gaze, I poised the needle above his neck.

"My hands are shaking," I said to Alexandre. "I can't do this."

"You can, Maisie." Alexandre was calm, positive. "One quick, hard push into the neck muscle and then inject the fluid! Keep talking to him the whole time. You're doing great!"

I took a deep breath; I looked at Claude and then, with my heart pounding, I thrust then needle deep into his neck!

Claude put his ears back and shook his head in anger

at the pain, but he didn't bite me. I injected the fluid and pulled the needle back out again.

"Done it!"

"*Bien!*" Alexandre was delighted.

It was enough for him for one day, the vet told Alexandre. The antibiotics would see him through the night. Tomorrow he would come back and he would sedate Claude and examine the leg properly. If I could be here then, that would be useful, to help control him.

"Of course I'll be here," I told Alexandre. I knew now that I couldn't leave Claude's side. The horse needed me.

When Nicole came to visit me that night to see if I was ready to come home, I told her I was staying. "I'll sleep here," I said.

She agreed to bring me a sleeping bag and some dinner and a change of clothes and, as she was leaving, I looked at Claude, asleep now in the straw, the pain and exhaustion having overwhelmed him at last, and I called to Nicole before she went.

"Please," I said. "Could you bring me my easel too, and my stack of canvases and my paints and the bag that contains my sketch book?"

That bag, I knew, contained Rose's diary too. I would

read it late that night when I couldn't sleep. I would be exhausted from painting by then – I'd be working for hours and hours until well past midnight.

\*\*\*

As I picked up the diary much later that night, I could see that my hands were covered in oil paint and my fingers were red from holding the brush so tight for so long. But it was worth it because on the canvas before me I could see the beginnings of my portrait of Claude. I had painted him just as he lay before me there on the straw of the stable floor. I painted everything, the froth of sweat on his neck, the terrible gash on his leg, the sinew and the bone. All of it was exposed, but what the portrait truly laid bare went deeper still. For the first time in my work, I was seeing the heart of a horse. Claude, so brave and so heroic, was fighting a great battle, and the dark spectre of death was looming over him, so close that I could feel its presence. In death's shadow, I couldn't sleep. So I curled up in my sleeping bag and opened the diary to the page where I had left off before, returning once more to the watery wastelands of Flamants Roses.

CHAPTER 12

## *Wild Horses*

*May 10, 1853*

The light in the Camargue is not the same as in Paris. The sky is as soft as a watercolour, the dusky grey clouds on the horizon bleeding into the pale, pearly waves of the sea. It is this light that defines my painting now. The oil colours that I once relied on – the mustards and the browns, the dirty umbers that once created my world, all remain untouched in their tubes and instead I use different paint tones – chalky whites and dove greys, deep teals and muted greens.

I am painting every day, rising early to greet the dawn. I always think I will be the first one up, but in the kitchen

Mimi is already there waiting for me, dressed in her uniform of jodhpurs and a cotton blouse.

"I have your breakfast, Rose," she will say. "One egg or two?"

And I say, "Two, please." Two fried eggs but no sausage because I am vegetarian – which Mimi still struggles with – and a brioche and café au lait. I eat mine while she takes Chantal's breakfast upstairs to her on a tray to eat it in bed.

I never need to go upstairs. Mimi has converted the old library downstairs into a bedroom for me and there is a bathroom right beside it. My wheelchair slips in beside my bed and I've learnt to roll myself out of bed and straight into it, and then to wheel into the bathroom to wash my face and brush my teeth. Mimi has installed a wooden rail by the toilet so that I can lift myself on to it and then back to my chair.

"You don't need me. You can do it yourself," Mimi tells me. She says the Camargue is no country for the weak, and life here will make me tough. She is right. I look back on the whining child I was in Paris and I cringe with shame.

I am a creature of the Camargue now, like the

flamingos and the bulls and the grey horses that roam the coastline, cantering in wild herds through the white froth of the waves. I see them in the distance sometimes. The Camargue horses are a perfect combination of power and beauty with burly physiques, strong legs and noble heads. They are untamed things and yet, twice a year, Pierre and the other gardians who work Mimi's farm will muster them into the yards and select out a few from the feral herd to turn into their riding horses for the next season.

Pierre has a very nice horse from one such muster – a stony silver-grey mare with very big round dapples on her rump and the most luxurious silken white mane you have ever seen. Her name is Babette, and she is very quiet, so she is perfect for her morning duties with me.

Pierre is ingenious. He has taken a wicker basket, the sort that the fishermen use to store their catch when they are at sea, and he has refashioned it into a seat of sorts, then padded the wicker on both sides so that it is soft against Babette's back and comfortable for me to ride in. He straps the seat to her saddle-back with leathers so that it sits sideways like a tiny armchair on Babette's broad rump. Pierre lifts me up to sit in it, and then he vaults up in front of me to sit astride in the saddle, and in this way, at a steady walk, we set off through the salt marshes, bound for my destination.

So this is how I ride a horse now. In a basket on the back like I am some groceries being carried from market.

When I'm asleep at night I dream that I am riding astride like I used to do. I'm galloping hard and fast on the back of a grey horse through the waves on the beach, and I can feel the thrill of the horse moving underneath me and the wind in my face blowing back my hair from my eyes and then I'm falling and I slide down off the horse's back and before I hit the ground . . . I wake up. And I feel down through the blankets with my hands and I touch my legs and they are, of course, still numb and lifeless and it was all just a dream.

Pierre tours me around the whole estate of Flamants Roses, taking me to different parts of the farm so that I can find things to paint. Right now my favourite place is in the grasslands near the salt water flats. This is where the flamingos stalk the salty estuary. Salt-water beavers swim past, and sometimes a pond turtle pops his head up. The salt-poisoned land is bare except for the hardy marsh grasses and spindly tamarisk trees.

When Pierre reaches the expanse of high ground where the marsh grass grows thick, he halts Babette and first lifts me down, then unpacks my things: the canvases and the easel and my paints, and my lunch that Mimi has packed for me. Cheeses and baguette and a peach picked from her tree. He puts it all down beside me and then mounts Babette once more.

"Work hard!" he tells me as he wheels the mare and sets off at a canter through the marsh water. And I watch him go until I can't see him any more, and I'm all alone in the middle of nowhere. Then I set up my canvas and I begin to work.

At the moment, I am intrigued by painting the flamingos. I'm using watercolours when I begin to bring them to life: cadmium red and scarlet to do their feathers, with chalk white blended in to capture their softer tones, and vermillion for their legs. They are such amazing creatures with ridiculous proportions. Their long necks and bulbous beaks should make them comical, but instead, they possess a mystery and an elegance of form that fascinates me.

The hours fly past as I work. Sometimes, I even forget to eat the lunch. The sun beats down hot in the afternoon, but I keep painting and then, before I know it, the day is over. The sky at the horizon is turning the colour of warm honey, and I hear hoof beats in the distance and I know Pierre and Babette are returning for me.

Pierre will leave Babette to graze beside the tamarisk trees and he will come to look at the easel to check my progress. He always has something smart and useful to contribute. Perhaps he'll say, "There's not enough action happening in this corner" or even more direct, "The beak on that flamingo in the middle is oddly misshapen". He is often right, and so in spite of the fact that he makes me cross, I do listen.

He washes my brushes out for me while I pack the rest of my things. And then he loads me on the back of Babette along with my easel and the canvas strapped so that the paint won't smear, and we journey home. This is how my days go. Or at least it was how they went. Until yesterday. Yesterday, Pierre deposited me on the grass by the tamarisk as usual, and I was beginning a new canvas, watching the flamingos as they fluffed up their feathers and stretched their legs in that long, absurd gait they do to wade the marshes. Then, out of the blue, the birds were startled and, in an ugly flap of wings, tried to elevate themselves. Their frantic efforts made them look like they were running on the surface of the marsh.

Eventually, ungainly and ridiculous, they took to the air. And the reason for their escape became clear a moment later. There was a herd of wild Camargue horses coming our way, cantering through the water in a direct line for the place where the birds had been just a moment before.

They were the most amazing sight. There were twelve of them in total. I counted twice over to check their number. It was hard to be certain because they all looked so alike! All of them the whitest shades of grey, with faint rosy dapples on their rumps and their eyes dark and muzzles sooty. Their tails were so long that they dragged in the salt waters behind them as they slowed to a trot, flicking mud on to their bellies as they ploughed through the water. The estuary was at mid-tide and the sea was up to their knees, and they moved through it as if they were a part of the water themselves.

Then the horse at the head of the herd spooked at the sight of me in the long grass ahead and she halted dead with her head raised high. She was large and imposing but clearly female as she did not possess the thick crest of neck that marks out the stallion in a herd.

It's funny how people who do not know horses always

think the stallion must be the one in charge, but in fact, the lead horse is nearly always a mare. Her job is to keep the other mares in line and look for danger. So was I danger? She certainly stared hard at me for a while longer, and then she left the rest of the herd, who had come to stand behind her, and stepped slowly through the marsh water, approaching the grassy outcrop where I sat. I could see her nostrils working like bellows, taking in my scent on the sea air, trying to decipher whether I was a threat. She sniffed and she stared and then, satisfied that I wasn't going to cause trouble, she dropped her head down and began to graze on the marsh grasses quite near me.

On her cue, the other horses in the herd began to graze around me too and soon I was in a magical circle, surrounded on all sides by these incredible grey marshhorses. I could see now that the lead mare herself was pregnant. Quite fat with a foal in her belly, in fact. And she was not the only one. Two other mares were heavy with foal. A couple of mares did not appear to be in foal, and the others were too young to be breeding stock, two yearling colts, three fillies and a pair of stallions. Of the stallions, it was clear that one was the sire, the more powerfully built and older of the pair. The other stallion was his second-in-command, and they did not fight, indeed they appeared quite the companionable pair, grazing on the outskirts away from the mares and the young ones, keeping watch and raising their heads constantly to listen for any enemy or smell any danger on the ocean air.

For the rest of the day I was absorbed in my work as I painted the herd while they grazed around me. And at dusk, the lead mare rallied them by snapping and baring her teeth, and they set off once more at a canter through the marshlands. By the time Pierre came to take me home, they were gone and I was alone. But I had captured them on my canvas and I rode back to Flamants Roses with Pierre and Babette feeling light-headed with joy. This is much better than painting flamingos.

*May 17, 1853*

A week has gone by since my last diary entry, I see. Things have changed. The herd no longer fear me, and even the young colts will graze right up close beside me. I caught one of them today with his muzzle covered in paint from sniffing my palette! They are such curious creatures. I had to use my blouse to wipe his face clean.

The twelve, as I call them, are a tightly knit herd. The

three mares heavy with foal captivate me most, and the one that I think most beautiful is the lead mare. I like how she is broad through the rump and has a thick shoulder, but her proportions are somehow still elegant and she has a very pretty head with a dished muzzle – quite unusual for a Camarguaise. Oh, and there is such a swagger about her! She moves with an air of authority through the herd, and all it takes is for her to flip her ears flat back and the other horses, the two yearling colts in particular, scatter in fear!

As well as the two colts in the herd there are three fillies. I think one of the fillies might be the offspring of the lead mare, because they often stay close together and groom each other. I would say the filly is little more than a year old. She has lost her baby fluff but is still leggy and gangly with a tufty outcrop where her mane will one day grow and her coat is still dark – somewhere between charcoal and brown. In time, it will lighten to dapple grey and then to white like her mama.

I have started drawing the herd in my sketch book. I am working on an image with all twelve horses in the frame, their poses completely natural and realistic. My ideas are still just at the rough sketch stage, but I can see things coming together in a way that pleases me very much. Soon, hopefully, I will be ready to put the sketch book aside and begin to paint on the canvas.

## May 30, 1853

The herd has moved on, the grass is gone, and so now instead of them coming to me, I've had to go to them. Pierre tracks their location and each morning he takes me to where they are. I travel lightly these days, to make his life easier, with just a sketch book and my lunch. Because my aim is to create art that is much grander in proportion my canvases have naturally become bigger. The new work will be done on a canvas stretched almost three metres. Mimi and Pierre have set it up for me to paint. It's so huge it takes up the whole length of my bedroom! I am not painting yet, though – I am still sketching, making drawings every day in my book as I sit and watch the horses.

They've grown so accustomed to my presence – yesterday I was even emboldened to touch the young filly. She was sniffing around my lunch basket so I spoke softly to her and reached in to grab a peach.

"Here you go," I offered, holding my palm flat with the peach on it.

The filly took it and promptly dropped it. I had to pick it up and hold it instead and hope that her teeth didn't nip me as she nibbled on it. In the end she ate all around the stone and gobbled the whole thing. I have called her Jolie.

*June 10, 1853*

A foal! He was born last night, delivered during the storm. Mimi says that horses in the wild instinctively give birth on a night like that because they know the rain and the wind will hide the scent of the newborn and protect it from predators.

Last night, the wind had arisen and the dark clouds were brewing across the salt flats of the Camargue when I went to bed. I woke once in the night and saw the lightning flash and thought to myself, "I bet a foal will come." Sure enough, by the time I found the herd, he'd been born. I have called him Laurent. He is the most beautiful thing. Two of the mares remain very pregnant still, including the lead mare, whom I have named Loulou.

We need another storm to bring the foals out!

*June 15, 1853*

The second foal is a gorgeous little filly! This morning when I found the horses, quite near to Flamants Roses in a quiet field with a small grove of tamarisk trees, there was the mare with her new foal at foot. And most amazing of all, she was so proud of her new offspring, she came all the way up to me with her foal just so that she could show her off. I reached up from my sitting spot and patted the foal on the velvet of her nose. She was so soft, I felt my heart melt and then the foal, surprised at the affection of my touch, gave a little snort and bounced and frolicked about putting on a display for me that made smile long after the horses had gone.

The lead mare remains heavy in foal and her belly is enormous. I imagine she is quite exhausted with being pregnant. Each day I come to see her expecting her baby to be there at her feet.

In my bedroom tonight, I began to map out the ideas from my sketch book on to the big blank canvas. The painting is taking shape. I have a name for it now: *Grignons de Camargue*.

CHAPTER 13

## *The Black Bag*

I haven't left Claude's side for three days straight. I've slept here on a camp bed that Alexandre brought in for me. Well, I say I have slept, but really I find it impossible to sleep. I worry that if I close my eyes when I wake Claude will have slipped away from me. His life still hangs by a thread. The vet came again yesterday and dressed the wounds and gave him more sedative and painkillers to make him comfortable. Alexandre says the vet wants to move Claude to the clinic so he can X-ray the leg and operate. He thinks the leg is broken and that, as I suspected, there could also be internal wounds. Alexandre says the Master of Horses has to approve the surgery. I'm not sure what the delay is, but Alexandre seems very uncertain about it all.

155

Marcel has not been back since this morning. I worry that when he returns it will be to take Claude from me. Until he does, I am glued to Claude's side and all I do is paint and paint and paint.

When I lift the brush now, it's as if I am possessed by a fever. I feel light-headed, hot-cheeked and my pulse pounds at my temples as I pour my heart out on to the canvas.

The painting I'm making is almost two metres long, which is large but nowhere near as large as the canvas Rose used when she painted *Grignons de Camargue*. It must have been so hard for her, I realise now, being in the wheelchair. How did she do it? Because I find myself using my legs constantly, crouched and prowling like a big cat at the bars of a zoo enclosure as I work my way along the canvas, back and forth and back again. My clothes become drenched in sweat as I work for hours on end without a break until, physically driven to the brink of exhaustion, I collapse on the straw and take in deep gulps of air and then I rise to my feet and I continue once more. My shoulders and my arms hurt. My hands can barely hold the brush. But there, in front of my own eyes, I can see it now. My painting is beginning to take shape.

It seems so long ago now – was it really just a few days ago that Françoise and I were in the Pompidou Centre? On the fourth floor there was an exhibition of a famous British artist. His name was Francis Bacon, and I had thought his paintings were terrifying. He painted people as though they had been turned inside out, their portraits as bloody and meaty as one of Rose Bonifait's trips to the abattoir. At the time, I thought his paintings were gross and ghoulish and yet I couldn't stop staring at them. Their darkness compelled me. Now, my own work shares that same bleak beauty. I paint with death looking over my shoulder. I can feel its talons grasping at Claude, clawing at his open wounds and proud flesh, trying to drag him down and away from me forever.

"He's going to die, isn't he?"

I put down my brushes and turn to find Françoise standing and watching at the stable door.

"I didn't hear you," I say. "Have you been there long?"

"Not very," she replies. "I came because I thought you must be hungry so I brought you this," she says, holding up a paper bag with a sandwich.

She doesn't move to step inside. She looks so pale and grim, and there are tears running down her cheeks at the sight of Claude.

"His wounds are very bad, aren't they?" Françoise says. And she asks me the question once more. "Is he going to die, Maisie?"

"I don't know," I say with brutal honestly.

Yesterday, I could hear Alexandre and the vet having an argument right outside Claude's stall. They were speaking very angrily in rapid French. I couldn't understand a word of it, but at the end I heard Alexandre say something to the vet and then the vet must have stormed off. When Alexandre entered the stall a moment later, I asked him what they'd been fighting about, but he shrugged it off. "We are both trying to do what is best for Claude," he said cryptically. He knows more than he is telling me, I'm sure of it.

"Claude can't die," Françoise says, and her words shake me out of my thoughts once more.

"If he dies, it's all my fault, you see? He saved my life. If it weren't for me, he wouldn't be here."

"It's not your fault," I tell her firmly. I want to tell her that Claude knew what he was doing and if he had the choice he would do it again. I am certain of it. "I know," I say. "He put his life on the line for all of those people inside the glass pyramid of the Louvre. Claude saved them because he's a noble horse of the

Garde républicaine. Claude knew that it was his duty to protect the innocent. He's a hero," I tell Françoise. "And he did what he had to do."

Françoise nods, sniffles a little and then tries to bravely smile. "Can I see your painting?" she asks.

Until now the canvas has been hidden from her. I paint with my back to the rear wall of Claude's stall. Standing at the doorway Françoise cannot see anything except the back of the canvas frame.

"It's not ready," I say. "I'm not finished."

"Please?" she asks again. "Just a look?"

I hesitate. This painting is so private. Until now it has just been me and Claude, but I need to steel myself and allow the world in to see it too. The world – starting with Françoise.

I walk across and open the door to the stall and beckon her in and close it again behind her. Not that it needs to be shut, I suppose. Slumped on the straw, Claude is hardly likely to rise to his feet suddenly and bolt for freedom. He doesn't move at all as Françoise walks past him to stand behind the canvas.

Françoise stares at the painting, transfixed. She says nothing. I think she must hate it.

"It still needs work," I try to justify myself. And then

I hear her make a strange, strangled cry. "Françoise? Are you OK?"

She bursts into tears! And before I can begin to comfort her she is out of the door saying, "I have to go!"

In the silence after she is gone, I feel my heart pounding. My pulse is racing again and I begin to paint, as if working the brush against the canvas is the only way to strip the fever from my body. While I paint, I listen to Claude's breathing and how it has become so laboured, it is as if each breath is a struggle, a slow, final gasp. I fear the hesitation between breaths, but then I hate the sound of it too – it is filled with his pain.

I've been painting non-stop for hours now and I'm totally spent. I have no strength left in my arms. But it doesn't matter because the work is finished at last. I put my brushes down and stagger back and stare at it dumbfounded with exhaustion. And then it seems as if I have finished just in time because the door opens and Alexandre is there, and the vet is there too and he carries with him a black surgical bag like a doctor would use.

"Maisie," Alexandre says. "We need to talk."

His words hang like the blade of a guillotine. I can feel the air in the room around me turning cold.

"What's in the bag? What are you doing to him?" I say to him.

At this moment the vet begins to speak to Alexandre in French and I don't understand a word of it and then Alexandre snaps back at him, also in French.

"What's he saying?" I ask Alexandre. "What's going on? Tell me!"

"He says the leg is very likely broken," he admits. "And there are internal injuries too and Claude is very hard to manage. And surgery is very expensive and seldom succeeds. The horse may never be ridden again."

"I know all of this," I say. "I've heard it before. But what else is he saying to you?"

"The vet has discussed Claude's situation with the Maître de Chevalier – the Horse Master here at the Garde. The Horse Master's job is to manage the Garde républicaine, and he says we are not in the business of rehabilitating injured horses, especially ones that have no chance of returning to full duties ever again," Alexandre says. "The Horse Master says that to keep Claude alive now is both inhumane and a waste of resources. If Claude cannot return to active duty as a ridden member of the Garde then it is the Horse Master's opinion that he should be euthanised."

161

My head is pounding. My heart thumps so hard in my chest, I can feel it inside me like it's fighting to get out.

"Murdered?" My voice is shaking.

"Not murdered. Put down. Maisie, it is the humane thing to do," Alexandre replies.

"Do you really believe that?" I say, with undisguised fury in my voice.

"It is not for me . . . it is the Maître who is in charge. And the vet says this is the only way."

"And what does Oscar say?"

Alexandre looks at his boots. "He doesn't know."

"Alexandre! You haven't told him?"

I look at him in disbelief. "Claude is Oscar's horse! You have to tell him and he'll stop the Master."

"Claude doesn't belong to Oscar." Alexandre shakes his head. "The horses here are the property of the Célestins. The Garde républicaine can do whatever they want."

"Oscar should know!" I persist. "He would want to be here. You know he would. He's your friend, Alexandre, please do it for him? Give Claude one more day so that Oscar can be fetched from the hospital to be at his side at least if you're going to do this."

Alexandre looks hard at me, pursing his lips. "Oscar is recovering from brain surgery and cannot be seen. And meanwhile, the horse is suffering."

"Give him one more day." I stand firm.

Alexandre nods. "OK, Maisie. I'll try. But I am not the decision maker."

He turns to the vet. They speak French once more, this time in hushed tones, although I don't know why they bother as I don't understand any of it anyway. Then the vet shakes his head, argues back, moves over closer to his black bag, which is lying on the straw of the stable floor. And I think he is going to open it, but he doesn't. He picks it up and gives me a nod and leaves.

"I'm going now to the hospital," Alexandre tells me. "We've won Claude another twenty-four hours, and if they will allow me inside, I'll tell Oscar what is going on. After that, we must act. Claude is in pain, and we have to think of the horse and do what is right."

***

*Do what is right.* Alexandre's words hang in the air after he leaves. Am I being selfish now? I don't want Claude to die. But he is suffering. I can see it. I have painted

163

his pain on my canvas and I know that his wounds are very bad. The vet thinks it's hopeless. Alexandre too. So what right do I have to do this to him? Perhaps I –

"Maisie!"

Nicole is at the stable door. She isn't alone. She has a man with her. He wears a beige trench coat and a shirt and tie. He is a funny-looking sort, inquisitive like a rat; bright eyes behind black-rimmed spectacles, short-cropped mouse-brown hair cut so close to his head it looks almost like he is bald. He carries a camera slung over his shoulder and a notepad in his hand.

"Nicole!" the sight of her makes me well up with tears. "Alexandre was just here. He says the Master of Horses, the head of the Republican Guard, is going to kill Claude!"

"What?" Nicole is horrified. "They can't!"

"Alexandre says they have no choice!" I say. "He had the vet with him with the black bag and everything. The Master, the head of the Guard, says they have to. They won't pay for him to have surgery and Claude is very sick and the leg is probably broken and he's being difficult to treat and they are horrible! Horrible!"

"Calm down, Maisie, calm down. It will be all right," Nicole says, but she looks like she might cry too.

"They want to have the horse put down?" The man in the black spectacles speaks with a London accent like mine!

"I put them off," I say, "but only until tomorrow."

The man looks over the stable door at Claude.

"But this is the horse that stopped the van," he says. "Do they realise they're about to kill a national hero?"

"They don't consider him a hero," I say. "To them, he's just a horse."

"Well," the man says with great assurance, "I think we can change that."

I am baffled. And then Nicole speaks up. "I'm sorry Maisie, I haven't introduced you. This is David Fisher. He is a reporter for the *International Tribune* newspaper. He phoned to interview me about Françoise and what happened at the Louvre and then we got talking about Claude and the painting that you are doing of him. I brought David down here because I think perhaps he can help us."

I don't see how this man can help. We have twenty-four hours. Claude has been given a death sentence. But I know better by now than to underestimate Nicole Bonifait. She has come here with a plan.

"You are going to tell David your story, about what

happened that day at the Louvre," Nicole says. "And then he'll take a picture, of you and of Claude and of the painting."

And then she explains her scheme to me, and I have to admit, it is brilliant. But we are running out of time. Tomorrow is the day that they will take Claude from me forever. We have to put our plan in motion and I can only hope it works.

***

That night, alone again, I pack my paints and I lie down in the straw beside Claude. I can hear his breathing, rasping and low, as I stroke his mane and I whisper goodnight to him. I'm going to leave his stall this time and go home and eat dinner, have a shower, resort to reading Rose's diary at 3 a.m. when I cannot sleep . . .

"I'll see you tomorrow, Claude." I give him a kiss on his forelock and stand up to go. And I promise him this will not be the last goodbye, but as I shut the door behind me, I worry that my promise is a lie.

## CHAPTER 14

# *The King Tide*

**20 July, 1853**

I write in this diary now shivering and shaking, frozen to the bone and harrowed to the core but counting myself lucky to be alive. The events of today, I must get down on paper while they are still fresh in my mind – for they have changed my world forever.

It began with the tides. I had noticed over the past days that the swell of the high tide was growing much higher than usual. Each day when the sea swept in, it kept on going, higher and higher, way above the usual tide marks, until it was flooding the estuaries and swamping the rice paddies and the marshlands so that the landscape was underwater and utterly unrecognisable.

"Late spring is the season of the king tides," Mimi explained. "A natural phenomenon. The cycles of the moon cause the sea to swell much higher than usual. You must be wary when you travel now because the waters can deepen further than you expect. Tides here in the Camargue have always ruled the land, and they can be treacherous."

This morning the sky was red, which is a sure sign of bad weather, and Mimi had suggested perhaps it might be wiser to stay home today and paint. But I was determined to go outside. I hate to be cooped up. I promised her I would not stay out all day and would get Pierre to bring me home in time for lunch. I was ready for a fight over this, but she seemed satisfied with my plan.

"The storm won't arrive before then," she said, eyeing the skies with a confidence of someone who has spent a life here in the Camargue reading the weather.

Pierre was in a sullen mood, partly because of the inclement weather and also about being sent out to herd back three black bulls that had escaped their pens. Even though he admitted to me, as we set off, that it was his fault they'd got free! He had left their gate unlocked.

"They are idiot creatures, escaping in such bad

weather," he griped. "And now we are out here too, and why? We should both be indoors!"

"I think stormy weather is exciting," I insisted. There was no rain yet but already in the distance the clouds were rolling black towards us and there was an ominous rumbling. Suddenly, a fork of lightning flashed against the rose-grey streaks of the clouds and Babette gave a most fearful whinny and almost bolted! Pierre had to clutch at the reins to stop her.

"To be out riding with a storm brewing isn't exciting! It's madness!" Pierre snapped at me. His complaints were thankfully lost on the wind from there on in as the weather worsened. Pressed up against his back, perched in my ridiculous little basket like a pet monkey, I didn't bother to try to speak as the headwinds whipped my words away as soon as they left my mouth.

As we rode on, I stared out at the horizon, watching the way the sky tinted as if it were a stained-glass window in a great cathedral, and the way the clouds shifted shape and rolled in the wind like tumbleweeds. I had never seen so many colours in the landscape, nor the light so extraordinary. I wished I had my paints on hand, instead of just a sketch book. I closed my eyes to try to imprint the coloured image into my memory so that I could paint it when I got home again. I even began to match the hues in my mind with the colours in my palette, mentally dipping the brush a little here and there to recreate the sky on my imaginary canvas.

"The sky is so pink!" I said to Pierre. "And that cloud there, it looks like a flamingo!"

"It looks like a storm, that's what it looks like!" Pierre was not in the mood for my romantic nonsense. And, possibly to avoid speaking to me any longer, he urged Babette on into a canter, and the wind against our faces got even fiercer and made it impossible to say another word as we headed for the marshlands.

Over the past weeks the grass had regrown in the coastland where I had first encountered the herd. The new growth had lured the horses back again. Pierre saw them back there grazing the day before, so he was almost certain that we would find the horses there again today.

"You must promise to be careful around them today," Pierre lectured me. "Don't take risks or get underfoot. Storms always make horses crazy."

As if to prove his point, Babette, who is a very sane mare, began skittering about beneath us as if there were snakes in the water at her feet – which for all I knew there were. The looming storm was making all creatures change their nature. The birds, apart from the flamingos, had taken to the skies and headed out to sea to ride out the worst of the weather.

To me, being out at sea looked utterly terrifying! I could see the surf roiling and churning on the coastline like an angry monster. Waves rose up like a sheer cliff face of grey-green water to toss and crash in a froth of turmoil on to the sand and then push their way higher and higher up the beach. And the estuarine tide came in around Babette's knees now, encroaching on the marshlands, the water levels creeping higher and higher.

The Camargue horses, though, were accustomed to the sea beneath their hooves. They spent their days knee-deep in the wild surf, their whiteness merging into the white froth of the crest of the waves. They knew how to scout for dry land to stand on, and now the wild herd had found the elevated plain of the marsh grass they were content to weather out the storm.

"See?" I pointed to the horses up ahead grazing on the grasses. "It's still dry here. I'll be fine."

But Pierre was not so convinced.

"I'm not leaving you," he growled at me. "Do your sketches. I'll wait."

"How are you going to fetch the bulls if you have me

on board?" I pointed out to him. "Pierre, it makes sense to leave me. I can draw the horses for an hour or two, you corral the bulls and then when you are done you can come back to fetch me."

Pierre objected further, though, refusing to give in to my plan. "Where am I supposed to even put you down? This ground, the marsh grass that we stand on, it will all be under water in a matter of hours!"

"This grass is always above sea level," I said. "I've never seen it underwater. And by the time you've mustered your bulls and returned for me I'll be done!"

I began to unbuckle myself from my chair so that Pierre had no choice but to dismount and lift me down.

He sat me on the driest patch of grassland he could find, not far from where the horses grazed.

"I'll be back in two hours," he said as he mounted. I waved him farewell as he cantered off through the water then turned my focus to the horses. They were entrancing to watch. Their behaviour had been intensified by the stormy weather, and there was a wildness and drama to their movements, the way they swished their tails and shook out their manes. I took out my sketch book and captured two colts rearing up in battle, hooves flailing at each other. And then the stallions, with their powerful necks crested and arched as they trotted the perimeter of the herd, guarding their precious mares against an unknown and unstoppable danger that they sensed all around them. I did a sketch of them too.

The mares were less active. They stuck close to their foals, but they did not really graze much, I noticed – they were too anxious. And Loulou was acting particularly oddly. She kept sniffing at her flanks and she refused to stay still, pacing about and raising her muzzle to the air with nostrils flared, trying to catch the scent of a predator on the wind. I was sketching her as she did this when she gave a funny little shake of her mane and then, suddenly, she dropped to her knees and lay down. She was flat on the ground and now she gave a grunt and thrashed about on her side and then stood up again and shook her whole body.

As I watched her, she repeated this once more. This time she lay flat on the ground and didn't get up again. Then she kicked at the air with her hind legs.

"Loulou? What's wrong?"

Loulou cow-kicked at her own belly with a hind leg and rolled over in the grass, flipping one way and then the other. Then she lay on her side, and let out a miserable groan. I looked at the protrusion of her enormous belly, rising up like a whale in front of me and I *knew*. Once, in our stables at Fontainebleau, one of the Thoroughbred broodmares had birthed a foal and my papa had woken me from my bed and taken me out to the stables so that I could watch it happen. Now, I was seeing the same familiar signs of a mare in labour and I knew: Loulou was about to foal.

But what a time and a place to have a baby! All around us the wind whipped mercilessly and the rain was beginning to fall from the storm clouds that boiled and seethed above us. How could nature be this perverse? And then I remembered what Mimi had said about mares giving birth in a storm so that the weather would mask the smell of the foal. The tempest would act as a protector and give the newborn a chance to rise to its feet and suckle without fear that predators might scent it on the air and attack.

This birth was hardwired into Loulou by nature. Her sudden labour in the storm was a bloodright handed down from her ancestors. And now, from here, everything would happen very fast. Horses were quick to deliver their foals. That Thoroughbred mare I had watched in the stables at Fontainebleau had given birth in a matter of minutes, not hours. Loulou's delivery would be quick too.

Except it wasn't.

Almost half an hour passed as I watched her heave and strain. She stood up several times over this period, kicked at her belly as if confused and then dropped to the ground again. And nothing happened.

When a whole hour had passed by and there was nothing to show for it, I began to panic. Her coat by now was drenched with sweat from her efforts. Sometimes she would raise her head to sniff her belly, or kick at her belly with a hind leg. She was in great discomfort, I could see that. The foal should have come by now, but there was no sign of anything emerging yet.

I looked to the horizon, hoping that Pierre might be done with the bulls and be returning for me, but there was no sign of him either. And now, Loulou was giving pitiful whinnies of distress. The foal was not coming out.

As if the weather wanted to speed matters onwards, the clouds were closing in, sweeping darkly across the skies to gather above us and the rain began to fall harder, sweeping down in bitter sheets. Soon it had soaked me to the skin and my sketch pad was utterly ruined. Not that I cared as I was no longer interested in my drawings, my entire focus had become Loulou and her unborn foal. The mare was still flat on her side, but she was no longer heaving and straining. She was lying utterly motionless and I would have thought she was dead except I could see her belly faintly rising and falling. She was breathing still, but exhaustion had beaten her and she had no energy left to push the foal out. She could not deliver it on her own. And I thought of the alternative – that if she did not give birth then both mother and baby would die like this. There was nobody here to help her.

Except, there was me.

But first of all I needed to get to her, and how was I going to do that?

There was only one way, and that was to crawl. I threw myself forward, propelling my body with all my strength so that I fell down hard, face-first, into the grass. I tasted dirt and choked a little on it. And then I pushed myself up on my arms, and surveyed the distance between myself and the mare. It was maybe four horse-lengths to get to Loulou from where I now lay. Not so very far. Yes, I could do this.

My legs were a dead weight as I dragged them behind me, crawling like a soldier in the trenches. I slithered on my belly, using my elbows to lever myself, trying to keep my momentum and inching forward on my forearms. With each drag I felt the grass poke and scratch me through my wet clothes, digging into my elbows, arms and stomach as I pulled myself across the ground. Soon, the cloth of my shirt had been ripped away and I was crawling on my bare skin. Pain shot through my arms as I put one forward and then the other, time and again, inching and inching. It was so slow! Was I even getting closer to Loulou? And then, I began to see my progress. With every painful belly slither, I was getting nearer. One arm in front of the other, brace, drag, pull, do it again. Until, at last, I was there, right behind the hindquarters of the mare.

"Loulou!" I was panting, exhausted. My arms were bloody and grazed, but I had made it. "Loulou, be brave . . . good girl, I'm just going to slip my hand up here to feel inside you . . ."

I pushed aside her tail, and then as I put my hands there I felt the mare kick! Loulou, startled by my touch, had lashed out and struck me in the shins! The kick was hard and it was square against my legs. For all I knew it had broken a bone. Yet I didn't feel it. My legs, after all, were already numb and paralysed. So it didn't hurt at all and I carried on. I spoke soothing words to her and I pushed, harder this time with my fingers, so that a moment later I felt my whole hand enter the birth canal and then my forearm had gone inside the mare.

Very gently, I began to feel where I expected the foal to be. A foal is born front feet first. So I should have been grasping for a front hoof. But that wasn't what I felt at all. The foal must have turned the wrong way so that it lay sideways twisted in her belly, creating a breach. No wonder she couldn't deliver like this!

I took my arm back out and thought hard on what to do next. I would have to turn the foal somehow while it was still inside her so that I could get it out. I elbowed my way forward once more so that now I was moved a little closer to Loulou's hindquarters. It was a precarious position. If she kicked out now she would strike me clean in the guts and that would hurt, possibly it would even kill me. But I needed to reposition myself like this if I was to be effective. Now, carefully, talking to her all the while, I put one hand inside to grasp at the foal and then pushed the other arm in too.

I had two things in my favour, I realised. The first was the size of my hands – tiny and slender, the hands of an artist – so I could reach inside and navigate to the foal. The other crucial factor was my knowledge of anatomy. Those days at the abattoir had given me a profound understanding of the internal workings of the horse. It was as if my eyes could look through Loulou's skin to see inside, to know exactly what I was dealing with here. I could do this.

I reached deeper with my left hand and at the same time I pushed with my right, trying to turn the foal, to move it from breach so that I could . . . ah ha! I had a foreleg in my left hand! I was sure of it. I pulled, not too hard, be careful, move just a little, still pushing with the right. The foal was turning further. I could grasp a second foreleg now. I took one leg in each hand and I pulled. Two tiny hooves emerged, trapped inside a rubbery white sac. Through the opaque membrane I could just make out the dark shape of the foal inside the birthing sac, a tiny head, the muzzle and the ears and then the neck and shoulders. And then . . . in a mad rush the foal's hindquarters slithered out, and I was caught up with it, the foal and me in a wet, fetid heap on the ground. I had been right in the path of the foal and the creature was now lying on top of me. I remembered back to the birth in the stables at Fontainebleau, how my father had helped the newborn foal to breathe by rupturing the birth sac to let the air inside. I needed to do this too as this foal's sac hadn't ruptured, and it was still trapped in its protective milky membrane. If the foal didn't get the sac torn, then it couldn't breathe. Except with the foal lying on me like this, I couldn't move.

I tried to wriggle my body out from the beneath the foal, but it was too heavy! And so I focused on moving just my right arm. If I could free it, then I'd be able to rip the membrane and clear the foal's air passages with my fingers. Squirming and contorting myself, I eventually managed to wrench the arm free. I grabbed the milky membrane with my trembling hand and found it surprisingly strong! It took a few tries before I had ripped a large enough hole that I could see the wet, dazed foal nestled inside the sac. I put my fingers up its nostrils and inside its mouth to make sure the airways were clear. Then I waited for what seemed like a lifetime for its breathing to begin, and just as I was panicking that it would never come, I saw the creature startle with a gasp. The foal had awoken! It began to take in air and then its eyes opened, deep brown pools, lashes fluttering. It was alive!

And I could sense my own breath now that the panic was over for the foal and I realised I too was having trouble breathing. The foal was lying directly on top of me and its not-inconsiderable weight was crushing my ribcage. I squirmed and pushed, struggling to free myself, and managed to get a bit of leverage and wedge myself forward, just enough to get my ribs clear and the air back in my lungs to breathe again. But that was all the movement I could muster. I was still trapped beneath the foal.

I was wondering what to do about this when the foal solved the problem for us both. It was alert now, and going through its own natural struggle. It's instinct for a horse to try to stand from the very moment it is born. This foal was no different, and now that it could breathe, its only mission in life was to get on all fours. The foal struggled against my legs and belly, four legs splayed akimbo, trying and failing to rise up. As it struggled, I squirmed too and in a brief moment when our struggles worked in unison, it made just enough space for me to crawl out from underneath and drag myself out by my elbows.

Panting and heaving, I pulled myself clear and then I managed to turn back to watch in wonder as one of the most remarkable miracles of nature unfolded before me.

It takes a human baby perhaps a year to find their feet. A newborn foal can find theirs in less than thirty minutes. So it was that I watched as the foal – a colt, a baby boy – developed his ability to rise up and stand erect before my very eyes. He began by splaying his four legs awkwardly, failing and falling time and again, lurching forward, stumbling, crashing. Loulou, meanwhile, was also getting back to her feet. She was exhausted too, but she was so proud to have birthed him! She was whinnying encouragement to the foal and she'd begun to lick him dry, cleaning his coat of the mucus and muck of the delivery. But the rain fought back her efforts to dry him. It was falling heavily now and the endless downpour soaked the newborn to the skin. It soaked me too. I had goose bumps and was freezing. And all this time the seawater kept rising. It was creeping up the marshlands, so close that the waves were lapping at us. If the foal did not stand soon, he would be in the water. And then I realised with a chill that it was the same for me. The marsh grass I sat on was all but gone – I could only see the tips of the stalks poking up through the water.

I scanned the horizon for Pierre, but there was no sign of him anywhere. The storm was raging, the waves kept rising and I was alone, surrounded by an endless sea.

## CHAPTER 15

# *The Hammer Falls*

The next morning at dawn, I went to the newsagent across the street and bought a copy of the *International Tribune*. Claude, my painting and I were the cover story, our photograph above the article by David Fisher with a headline that read:

## TRAGIC END FOR HERO HORSE

In the story, David Fisher wrote about how Claude had saved the life of more than a hundred tourists inside the Louvre who had been in the path of the terror attack.

*Now,* he wrote, *we are repaying this national hero, this icon of French resistance, by ending his life.*

By mid-morning, the public outcry had reached a fever pitch. The radio news stations were filled with nothing else. Everybody was talking about the bravery of Claude and the injustice of his fate.

Nicole's phone started ringing at that moment. It was Augustin at the Paris Art School.

He had seen the picture on the front of the paper, he said. My portrait of Claude, from what little he could see in the newspaper photo, was quite different from my previous paintings. He liked it very much. And wouldn't it be appropriate and fitting if we were to move the auction schedule of lots and make space for it so that it could be sold tonight at Lucie's?

Yes, Nicole told him, yes it would. Her plan was coming together. She spoke again to David Fisher and he got busy writing a news update straight away. By midday the *International Tribune* had put a close-up picture of my painting on their website with the announcement that the painting of Claude the Hero was to be one of the lots in tonight's auction at Lucie's.

By afternoon the international media had picked up on this story too, and it had gone around the world. My dad phoned me.

"Your painting," he said, "is on the cover of *The Times*."

It's funny to think now that once upon a time, this would have mattered to me. I mean, what artist wouldn't want to see their painting make headlines around the world? But my art career was not what mattered now. I was still thinking about Claude and hoping that the rest of Nicole's plan would succeed.

Nicole had told me that Lucie's would be very fancy. I didn't have any clothes good enough, but Françoise had come to my rescue and lent me a dress. It was black with silver threads that frayed at the hem. She lent me shoes too, so I looked very much like the rich women who crammed the front rows of the auction room to take their seats. Except they held their bidding paddles in one hand and a glass of champagne in the other.

"It's good for the bidders to have champagne," Françoise muttered to me as a gaggle of rich old ladies fanned themselves with their paddles, "Maman says it loosens the purse strings."

In a cloud of blond-haired socialites on the far side of the room I saw Augustin. He was looking very arty and serious this evening. He wore a beret without a hint of irony, and while everyone else was in suits he was in paint-stained overalls, just to prove the point, I think, that he was a proper artist. It seemed quite pretentious to me. When he saw me across the room, he hastily drew the conversation with the posh ladies to a close and hurried over.

"I have been backstage to see Claude up close," he told me. And I thought for a moment that he meant the horse, but then I realised he meant the painting.

"Do you like it?" I asked him.

Augustin hesitated. "No," he said. And there was a vacuum, an airless moment between us. "I don't like it," Augustin said. "I don't think one can 'like' a work as powerful and important as this painting. I don't like it. I am in awe of it. It is the most exciting work of art any of my students has ever produced in the entire time I have been teaching at the Paris School."

At first I thought he might be mocking me. But then I realised Augustin had never made a joke in the entire time I'd known him. He was deadly serious.

"All this time," he said to me, "if I was hard on you Maisie, it is because I knew you had this inside you. You had such technique, such natural composition. Now you have found the grit and beauty that separates true art from mere decoration. I look at Claude and I feel the full impact of what it means to be alive, and to face down death and look it in the eye without fear. This work you have produced marks your potential as a future artist of greatness. I am humbled to have taught you."

I really didn't know what to say. Augustin, who had made my life so difficult since I had got here, was one of the good guys after all? As it turned out, I had no time to reply because the auction was now underway, and the auctioneer was announcing the first lot. As they carried the painting on to the stage I felt sick with fear that if I said another word or raised my hand I might end up buying something by mistake!

And so I kept my hands glued to my sides and my mouth zipped as Monsieur Falaise worked his way through the catalogue. He was so swift! The Lucie's auction staff had only barely finished carrying a lot up on to the stage to place on the easel before he got underway. First he would explain the work, naming the artist and making a few comments of his own about the art, then he would begin his mellifluous and rhythmical chanting, the auction patter, and the paddles would start rising and the numbers would keep climbing. And Françoise was at my side, driving me mad, translating anything I didn't understand, her own pattern echoing the auctioneer.

"What am I bid? Over there, sir! Well done, madame! Go higher, mademoiselle!"

Sometimes it was clear to me which works were worth the big money. The patrons in this room were here to buy statements that emphasised their own wealth – massive works that would look good in gilt frames hanging in their palatial drawing rooms. So the art that got the highest bids was big, bold and glamorous. Or at the very least it would look good matched up with your sofa.

"Ugh! Who would want that staring back at them?" Françoise said when the bidding went wild for a painting where a man had been given the head of a pig in place of his own face. Beside her, the art patrons turned to glare at the young girl with such loud opinions, but Françoise didn't care. She was fearless in the auction room and thought the whole affair was hilarious. A couple of times, she even raised her hand and placed a bid! At one point she 'borrowed' a paddle from a lady and nearly bought a painting by mistake – which I found terrifying and she found funny. Françoise, of course, had been attending these Lucie auctions since she was a baby in her mother's arms. To her they were entertainment to be enjoyed. But to me, it was so stressful! Lot after lot, I felt my pulse rising as I waited for them to reach my painting, and all I could think about was Claude.

What would selling his painting achieve now? The public outcry had been huge on his behalf, but the Célestins had been unwavering. It was not their policy to care for a permanently injured horse. Even with the groundswell of public opinion against them, they had held firm to their position that the humane thing to do would be to end Claude's life. It appeared that Nicole's plan to get the public behind us and demand that the Célestins change their mind would fail anyway. And now, here I was, spending Claude's final hours in a stupid room filled with rich, snobby women and their well-leashed husbands about to pay too much for paintings of squiggles and blobs and . . .

"Lot number sixty-seven!" Monsieur Falaise's cry silenced the room around me. "This substantial work, in oil on canvas, is entitled, *Claude*."

I could feel my heart hammering like mad in my chest. This was it! The moment had come at last.

"Who will open the bidding at five thousand euros?"

I couldn't believe what I was hearing! Five thousand euros? All the other works so far had fetched no more than two or three thousand. To open the bidding at this sum was –

"I have five thousand bid! *Alors*! We are underway who will give me six thousand?"

I was craning my neck, trying to peer round the backs of the people standing front of me to see now who was doing the bidding, but all I could catch was a glimpse here and there of a paddle being raised, and then the auctioneer pointing his long bony finger across the room to identify a new bid.

"With you, madame, at twenty-five, and with you now, sir, at twenty-six. Madame? You want to go higher? Thank you we have twenty-eight. Now twenty-nine . . ."

With each new bid I felt my heart thumping harder in my chest. Françoise was tugging at my sleeve now, gaping at me open-mouthed. Neither of us could believe what was happening in the room at that moment. And then, there was a brief lull, and the auctioneer surveyed the crowd and as he did so, the two men who had been standing in front of me blocking my view parted a little so that I had the painting of Claude clearly in my sights, and I saw my horse, the pain and agony in his deep, dark eyes. And I realised that what was happening in this room right now, it was ridiculous to me. I didn't care in the end how much money my painting made. All I cared about, all I had ever cared about, was Claude. So why was I here now when I should be at his side?

It was only once I turned to leave that I realised just how full the auction room had become. Behind me people were crammed in all the way to the door. There was no room to squeeze through and nobody looked like no one was going to move aside for me either.

"I'm sorry! I have to go!" I tried to elbow and push my way through but they barricaded me in! One woman glared at me and said something in French in a snooty tone. I could feel my blood boiling. I tried to part the crowd again, in French this time. "*Je suis desolé! Pardon, pardon . . .*"

*Oh, come on! Move!* "Please! I have to go!"

I was having trouble breathing now, the claustrophobia had kicked in and I was about to completely lose my mind and begin clawing at people like a wild animal when, like a miracle, the crowd directly in front of me suddenly parted and I saw Nicole.

"It's OK, Chou-chou!" She grabbed me by the wrist.

I mean really grabbed me. I felt her long scarlet nails dig into my flesh a little as she pulled me forward, easing me through the crowds. "Come with me now. I have you!"

She put her arm around my shoulder and I felt a bit like a celebrity being ushered through the paparazzi by their bodyguard. Nicole cut a slender figure, but her presence was formidable and there was something about her haughty demeanour that made people fall back and let us through. In a moment she had me out of the auction room and we were in the grand foyer and then on the marble stairs and tumbling together out through the elegant glass doors of Lucie's to emerge into the outside world.

Even out here, the pavements were busy, thronging with people who hadn't been able to fit inside the auction house. The café beside Lucie's was overflowing onto the pavement, with elegant couples sipping drinks.

"Take deep breaths, that's it," Nicole told me as I crouched with my head between my knees trying to get my equilibrium back. Then she grabbed a waiter from the café, spoke charmingly to him, and I saw him scurry off. A moment later he'd brought us back a chair for me to sit on and a tall glass of fizzy water for me.

"Here, drink this." Nicole passed me the glass and I knocked it back in a single gulp.

"I'm fine," I insisted.

"*Oui, oui, Petit Chou-chou Anglaise*," Nicole soothed, "but take a moment first to catch your breath."

"Do you feel well enough to go back inside now?" Nicole asked me. "This is your moment of glory. Your work is going to fetch a record price, I think."

I had thought she understood. "I'm not going back in," I explained. "I don't care about the painting. I want to go back to Claude,"

Nicole gave my hand a squeeze. "I understand completely," she said. "Who cares about a room full of bourgeoisie? Tonight of all nights, you should be with him, no?"

I felt bad to be running away. "I'm not being ungrateful, Nicole . . . I know how much this means to you . . ."

"Don't be silly, Chou-chou!" I felt her arms around me, smelt her heady oriental perfume as she embraced me. "Go to him now! We have done what we can but if these are truly to be his final hours, you should be at his side."

And then I was running, my legs like jelly underneath

me, lungs feeling like they would burst. All the way down the boulevard Henri IV to the gates of the Célestins.

Alexandre, of all people, was on guard duty.

"Maisie?" He dropped the newspaper he'd been reading. "I thought you were at the auction?"

"Alexandre, please? May I come in?"

Alexandre frowned. "You shouldn't be here, Maisie, not now . . . They will be coming for him soon."

He gave a sigh and reached beneath the desk of the sentry box, pressed the button and the automatic doors swung open.

"If the guards come, you make yourself invisible, yes?" Alexandre said. "You are not here."

"I am not here," I confirmed. "I am a shadow."

"That's my girl," Alexandre said. And then, with a wave of his hand, "Hurry now! A shadow moves quickly! Go to him!"

There was a moment, outside Claude's stall, when I could not bring myself to open the door. But what kind of friend would that make me if I could not confront whatever I found in that room? And so I slid the bolt and stepped into the gloom.

He was alive! And at the sight of me he raised his

head and gave a nicker. I fell to my knees beside him, saying his name, cradling his mighty head in my arms.

"I know you're in such pain, Claude," I whispered as I stroked his forelock. "But you won't need to be brave for much longer. I promise you, when they come for you, no matter how much it breaks my heart, I will stick by you. I'll be with you in the end. I promise, I promise . . ."

Footsteps outside in the corridor! Alexandre's voice and that of the vet and another man. I knew him by sight when the three of them appeared. He was the Maître de Chevalier. The Horse Master of the Célestins.

"Please . . ." I was about to beg them for more time, for one more chance to change things. But before I could, Alexandre was telling me something, words that took a moment to register.

"We're not here to harm him, Maisie. There has been word from above, from no less than the President of France himself. We've been instructed that Claude is to be taken immediately to the vet hospital and all their resources are to be placed at our disposal. The horse is to be saved at any cost."

I couldn't believe it. The publicity around the auction must have worked.

"Are you serious?" Tears were running unchecked down my cheeks. "Alexandre, is this for real?"

Alexandre dried my eyes, helped me up from the floor.

"It's for real," he said. "You did it, Maisie. You and Nicole and that journalist at the *International Tribune*."

He smiled at me. "Claude is a symbol of Paris now. Our eternal flame. And this is the will of the people of Paris. Claude must survive."

## Chapter 16

# *Gardians of the Camargue*

When the seawater had reached my waist, and the waves that kept coming now struck me as high as my chest, I became so cold that I couldn't feel my fingers any more. And the rain! It had been torrential before, but now it was driving down in a bleak grey cloak that smothered us. The rush of the wind and the roar of the sea was so loud that it filled my ears. So much so that I truly didn't hear the horse galloping hard towards us until it was almost too late. Then my ears pricked at the sound of the hoof beats and the cries calling my name, straining against the wind, Pierre's voice anguished and grief-stricken.

"I'm here!" I called back. "I'm alive! I'm here!"

And then, through the rain and the gloom, Pierre

appeared. His horse was still in motion as he threw himself from her back and ran to me, picking me up with his hands around my waist, dragging me out of the water. I must have weighed twice my usual amount, my clothes were drenched through and sodden with seawater. Thank God at least I don't wear foolish skirts and layers of petticoats, I was heavy enough to carry in my trousers. Pierre held me in his arms like a baby, clutching me close to him.

"You're freezing!" he said.

"I know that!" I stammered in reply. And he laughed at this, but it was a high-pitched anxious laugh. Because now that he had found me, our troubles were clearly not over yet. The waters were still rising.

"Where is Babette?" I asked. For I could see now that this horse was another grey mare from our stables.

"Babette is wounded," Pierre said. "It all went wrong. The bulls . . . I had trouble with them. They went wild. I was trying to control them and they charged us down. Babette got gored by one of them as we drove them through the gates. I had to ask one of the gardians to exchange horses with me and take her back to Flamants Roses while I came to look for you."

As he told me this he was holding me tight to his

chest, trying to use his body heat to thaw my cold bones. It was working. I could feel his heart beating hard against my own and little by little the feeling was flowing back into my fingers once more.

"There's no basket on your saddle," I observed.

"Can you ride astride, do you think?" Pierre asked hopefully. "I'll double you in front of me. This horse is a good one, she will get us home . . ."

I realised what he meant to do, to take me back with him now. "Pierre, I can't go," I said. "Loulou's foal is too weak to leave behind. If we abandon him in this storm, he will die."

Pierre looked over at Loulou who stood only a short distance from us, fussing over her new baby, but the rain was making him wet again as fast as she could lick him dry. As the wind drove the rain towards us in bleak sheets, she moved to use her body as a shield to protect her newborn from the elements as much as she could. But her efforts could not stop the floodwaters from rising. The storm had yet to reach its peak and the water was still climbing and showing no signs of receding. The foal had fed, and he looked alert and bright now, but it was only a matter of time before his young body succumbed to exhaustion. Newborn foals cannot remain on their feet

199

for long, they need to sleep. And when this foal lay down, he would be lost, he would take his last breath and disappear forever beneath the floodwaters.

"What can we do?" Pierre shouted to be heard above the storm. "The foal will not leave his mother's side. And we can't take him alone. He needs the mother, he has to keep feeding or he'll die."

I looked at Loulou. She was exhausted, by both the force of the elements and her own efforts to bring her reluctant foal out of her belly and into this world. Her tiredness was evident, and yet in her eyes there was still that same fire and spark there had always been. Her ears swivelled forward and back as she listened to us talk, as if she instinctively knew that her fate relied on us now. In these past months, my bond with Loulou had become so powerful, and I knew she trusted me, I was sure of it, and it would be that trust that I needed to rely upon now.

"Use your cattle rope," I said. "Take it from the saddle, knot it into a halter and put it on Loulou."

Pierre looked at me, confused. "You want me to halter the mare, not the foal?"

"The mare is accustomed to the hand of man. She is branded – which means she has been saddle-broken in the past, you said so yourself. She can be ridden and the foal will follow at her feet. If we can get Loulou home, then the foal will follow us and we save them both."

Pierre shook his head. "I cannot ride one horse and hold on to you and lead another horse all at the same time . . ."

"You won't have to lead her," I said. "I'll be riding her."

"But you cannot!" Pierre's reaction was immediate. "Rose! You have no legs."

"I have legs," I pointed out. "It's true that I cannot kick with them or hold on tight, but they will provide me with enough weight to balance myself. I can sit upright and stay on board. And if you give me a switch, a tree branch to use, I can tickle Loulou onwards instead of kicking."

"It's too dangerous," Pierre insisted. "You'll fall."

"Before I lost the use of my legs, I had an excellent seat," I told him. "I could ride bareback at a gallop."

I looked hard at him. "I have ridden horses my whole life, Pierre, do not presume to tell me I can't do this."

"I'll take you home and come back for them . . ."

Even as he said this, I could see Pierre knew it was impossible. He'd had enough trouble finding me. How would he find Loulou and the colt as the storm worsened. And how would they survive that long?

"Stop trying to think of another way, because there isn't one," I said. "There is only my way. Grab the rope now and make a halter and put it on Loulou. Every moment that we stay here and discuss it we only put ourselves in the path of the storm."

Loulou must have known we were helping her. She didn't object when Pierre stuck the rope halter on her head. Then he came back for me. I was freezing cold when he picked me up to lift me on to her back.

"Wait! what about the others?" I gestured across at the herd, standing knee-deep in the seawaters that were still rising.

"They will be fine, they are bred to weather such storms," Pierre assured me. I think he was worried I would come up with a new plan to take all of them with us!

With me in his arms, Pierre searched the floodwaters for a suitable stick and in the dark murk of the sea, he snatched up a slender broken-off branch of a tree.

"Your riding crop," he said. I reached out and took it, and it felt strange in my grasp since I had never been one to whip a horse before. I tucked the branch down my trousers so that I could use both hands to grip Loulou's mane.

"Get me up on to her back now," I told Pierre.

It was not elegant, I admit. Even though Loulou stood remarkably still, it took a shove and a push from Pierre to forcibly swing my dead right leg over the mare's back so that I had one leg on each side and sat astride.

When I sat up, I was aware of the strangeness of being on a horse on my own for the first time in a very long time! There was a brief moment in which I felt this miraculous joy swell in me. This sensation I was feeling now was one that I thought had been lost to me forever. I was riding! And then Loulou swung her hocks and moved suddenly to the left and I lurched and swung with her. As I gave a startled squeak, I realised this was no time for misty-eyed memories. I was on a strange horse in the middle of a wild storm and had every chance of being thrown headfirst into the sea with no way of keeping myself afloat if I fell. So this wasn't the time for fey daydreams, harking back to my old life. I had a task ahead of me, and I must not lose sight of it. It was up to me now to get my horse home.

"I'm all right," I assured Pierre. "You can mount up. I have her now and we will follow you."

Pierre ran to his mare, wading as fast as he could through the waves which now reached above his knees. He sprang up into the saddle, gathered up his reins and turned her into the prevailing storm so that he formed a blockade of sorts, taking the brunt of the weather ahead of us.

"Stay behind me!" he shouted over his shoulder. "It might shelter you a little."

Riding in this way, yes, he made a decent enough wind break. And because I had no time to think about it, I found myself immediately adjusting to my new riding style in which my makeshift riding crop served the purpose that had once belonged to my now limp and useless legs.

Loulou must have been broken in by a gardian at some point in her life, but she was still half-wild, as all the horses here are. And I was half the size of the gardians she must have been used to in the past, so she could have easily thrown me. But she didn't. I think she knew that we were trying to help her, because she kept me safe as we ploughed on together through the water. She understood the slightest shift in my weight or the touch of the makeshift reins, and I didn't even need a twitch from the switch to spur her on.

As for the foal, there had been a brief hesitation when we set off and he didn't quite understand that he should be coming too. Then Loulou gave him a commanding whinny, as if to say, "Hurry up, little one", and in a frantic gambol of skinny, ridiculously long legs, he gave chase. The waves were so high up on him that he had to do an ungainly waterbound canter to catch us up, and then within a few seconds he was at Loulou's flank, where he took his place tucked in tight against his mother.

In this way, a bedraggled caravan beset by the storm, we departed the submerged marshlands. As we traversed the watery coastline with the sea to the left of us the roar of the waves was deafening. The sea was still coming in and the tide had not yet reached its apex. We followed the shoreline, along the beaches, until we reached the swift-flowing waters that now surged inland through the rice paddies.

"Be careful!" Pierre called back to me over his shoulder as he entered the rice fields. "The water here is deep!"

And then we were plunging in and the seawater was all the way to Loulou's chest and I looked back and the foal was being pushed this way and that by the currents. He was such a plucky little fellow! I watched as he braced against the current and kept valiantly alongside his maman. Soon we were through the worst of it – we had entered the calm waters of the broader inland canals, the ones that Pierre had punted me along in his flat-bottomed boat when I had first come to live here, the day he had taken me out to meet Mimi and the gardians. Up ahead in the distance I saw the stables and the grey slate rooftops of Flamants Roses and I knew for certain at that moment that we'd made it! We were going to get Loulou and her foal home.

"There's Chantal!" Pierre exclaimed. And through the rain I saw her riding for us, mounted up on her horse Dante, waving and shouting with excitement.

"We've been out searching for you!" she cried. "When the gardians brought Babette back to us, we were so worried . . ."

She was soaked to the skin by the rain and her horse was flecked with foam and sweat. She pulled up along-side Loulou and threw her arms around me, hugging me, and then she realised.

"Rose! You're riding!"

"Rose!!"

Mimi was coming for us too now. She was on foot, running with the dogs at her heels.

"Get them inside the stables," she shouted at us,

struggling to be heard above the high winds of the storm.

It was so good to be out of the rain at last! Pierre unsaddled the horses and wrangled the foal and Loulou into a loose box together. Mimi mixed Loulou a hot mash and then made feeds for the rest of the horses and Chantal dug through the tack room to find a small woollen rug to put on the foal.

The storm had worsened by the time we left the stables and fought our way through the rain to reach the house, Pierre carrying me in his arms.

Inside the house, Chantal ran me a hot bath and my skin prickled in anger when it touched the hot water. I had been cold for so long, it seemed wrong to be warm again. I lay in the water and thawed out while Chantal prepared me some clothes. Mimi fussed and bustled in the kitchen so that by the time I was back in my wheel-chair, clean and warm and dry with rosy cheeks and a famished hunger, there was an enormous pot of hot bouillabaisse. The rich tomato soup was full of scampi and mussels and there was crusty baguette on the table too. We sat together, and while Pierre told our story to them, I spooned the bouillabaisse to my open mouth, because eating seemed more important than speaking at that point, although at times I would pipe up to correct his version of events, but mostly I ate and I laughed and I thanked my stars I was alive and I was home.

*July 23, 1853*

It has rained solidly for the past three days. I have spent my time in the shelter of the stables watching the progress of Loulou and the foal. Even though I am only gone for a few hours each night to sleep, when I return again I marvel at the changes that have taken place in him every day. He grows so fast! And no wonder, he drinks very greedily from his maman. Loulou is a good mother and puts up with his demands and his playful antics, but also like a good mare she knows when her son has crossed the line and then she rebukes him, with her ears pinned back, delivering a quick, powerful nip – hard enough for him to feel and know that his mother is displeased and so to behave himself. The nips come quite often because the foal is a very cheeky boy and they are stuck in close quarters here in their stall. Looking back, I think the foal's refusal to be born was the first sign of what may well be a troublesome nature. It is this miscreant streak that made me come up with his name. He is Sebastian – after my own first pony who was such a mischievous tyke in his own infamous way.

Each day, as Loulou and Sebastian grow stronger and the weather becomes settled and the king tides recede and the waters fall back, I know we are getting closer to the moment when we will have to let them go back to the herd.

"We cannot keep them too long," Mimi tells me. "To be stable-reared like this at this stage of his development will only turn Sebastian into a farm horse. To live on the Camargue he needs to learn resourcefulness. He needs to discover the wildness in himself."

And for the past three days I've nodded in agreement, and then I've said, "Just one more day, Aunty Mimi?" and she's smiled and said, "Very well, Rose, one more day."

And today? One more day I begged her. One more day, Aunt Mimi. Just for me.


*July 30, 1853*

The sun was out, the skies were clear and I saw the look on Aunty Mimi's face this morning when she handed me my brioche.

"It's time, Rose, we need to let them go."

Pierre had seen the herd grazing not far beyond our paddy fields just the day before. Loulou and Sebastian were well and getting more than a little restless in confinement. There were no more excuses I could make.

We rode out together, all four of us. Pierre was mounted on Babette, whose wound has thankfully healed. Chantal rode her mare, Eloise, Mimi was on Fabrice and I was on a young mare named Coco. That's right! I was on my own horse. And why not? I had proven in the storm that I could ride astride. So now, here I was, on horseback like the others. This time I rode with a switch in each hand to use instead of legs and because of this I couldn't lead Loulou. That task was handed to Pierre who ponied her along by her headcollar. Loulou stuck obediently behind him, and Sebastian ran at her feet, and we went almost as far as the place where the bulls are grazed in our outlying fields until we reached the point where the herd could be seen in the distance.

Loulou gave a whinny, a clarion cry across the fields. And then a moment later her exhortations were returned by another horse – one of the stallions beckoning her back to them. Calling to her to come home.

Pierre slipped off Loulou's headcollar and she didn't

hesitate. She galloped off from a standstill, her whinnies echoing through the Camargue marshes. Behind her, also galloping, Sebastian with his long legs, no longer ungainly, matched his mother's pace and her fluid strides.

"He will be quite the horse one day," Mimi said as she watched him run. "In perhaps three years from now, Pierre, we must bring him in with the muster and then he can become a good riding horse for Rose."

And then we headed home again, riding across the marshlands. Near to home we asked the horses into a trot for a stride or two. I am not bold enough yet to canter on my own, but when my balance improves it will come, I am sure of it.

## August 5, 1853

My life now has a routine. Each day I rise at dawn and I ride one of the horses out with Pierre or Chantal, and then I return and eat lunch and begin to paint. I have almost finished my grand work now, the painting that is three metres long and has dominated my bedroom and my life over the past year. It is very nearly done, and my new concern is that I might push it too far, add one more brush stroke where it doesn't belong and ruin it all. Aunt Mimi has just come in to look at the work, and I asked her what she thought.

"I have an art critic arriving tomorrow," she said. "He has a greater eye than mine. Let us wait and ask him."

An art critic? Coming here to Flamants Roses? Who can she possibly mean?

CHAPTER 17

## *Sold!*

One mid-summer afternoon in June, my dad and I took the winding footpaths through Kensington Gardens to the Georgian-style red-brick building that stood by the lake. It was a lovely walk, except for the bit where I had to make Dad stop and wait while I threw up in a hedge.

"Are you OK?" he asked me as I emerged from the bushes looking pale and strung out.

I nodded. "It's just nerves."

"You've got nothing to be worried about," Dad tried to reassure me.

But in truth he looked as sick as a dog too, and we both hesitated at that moment and stood on the path to catch our breath before I said, "Can we skip it and just go to McDonald's instead?"

Dad laughed. Then he put his arm around my shoulder and hugged me tight. "That would mean we'd miss your debut exhibition at the Serpentine."

"So that's a no?"

"They're all waiting for you, Maisie. Some of the most famous art critics in Europe will be there."

And that was when I had to duck into the bushes and throw up a second time.

It has been a year since I left Paris. And in that year my life has been extraordinary. After the auction at Lucie's, when *Claude* ended up selling for a colossal two hundred thousand euros, I became an instant superstar. For some kids, I guess the fame would have gone to their head. With me, it had the opposite effect. I felt like it had all happened too fast and I didn't deserve the accolades. I was worried that I had peaked in life at the age of thirteen! It would all be downhill from here!

Oddly enough, it had been Augustin who had helped me through that. My old art teacher who had been so tough on me in that term at the Paris School now became my greatest champion. At least once a week we would Skype each other and I would show Augustin what I was working on and he would critique my efforts, make suggestions and look over my virtual shoulder with the kind of clarity only an experienced artistic eye could provide.

My paintings continue to be large format, big oils on canvas, and since there was no way I could paint like that in our tiny flat, Dad helped me to rent an old garage space that had once been a car mechanic's, two streets along from our place in Brixton. It turned out there was quite a cool artistic community there, and I had other painters and people making films who were right next door. I paid for it myself, using some of my artist's portion of the auction price of the work that had sold at Lucie's. I hadn't realised at the time that, while the auction was for the college, the artist got ten per cent of the sale price at auction that day and for me that was twenty thousand euros!

I sold a few more works after that too. My bank account had all these zeros – or at least it did for a while. I'd spent a lot of it coming home from France. I had something very important to bring back with me, but I'll get to that story soon enough . . .

The Serpentine Gallery has always been one of my favourite places in all of London. When I used to come here to Hyde Park with Dad to work on those early paintings of horses, we'd often buy an ice cream and go and sit beside the attractive brick building and look out across the lake. It cost money to go inside, but sometimes if there was an exhibition of an artist Dad thought I would really like, then we'd pay the entry fee and go in.

This afternoon, though, I didn't have to pay an entry fee. Because I *was* the artist. And this was the opening of my show. The guests spilled out on to the lawns outside the pavilion as we approached and there were waiters pouring out glasses of champagne and handing around platters of fancy snacks. It was like the most glamorous garden party ever, and standing in the crowd, being more glamorous than any of them, was a woman in a gold leopard print gown with outrageous flowing red hair.

"Petite Anglaise!" Nicole Bonifait gave me a wave and strode across the lawn towards us with this wide smile. Behind her, Françoise, who had been prowling the platters of food, grabbed three puff pastries and raced behind her mother to join us.

"I've been inside already," Nicole told me. "There are red sold stickers on just about everything! It is just as well I chose my work over the video conference last week or I would have missed out entirely."

I felt like my knees were going to give way underneath me. "Seriously?" I said. "They've sold?"

"Of course they've sold!" Françoise chimed in through a mouthful of pastry. "Once the Chapman Gallery bought one, everyone wanted one."

"The Chapman Gallery?" I was stunned.

"Yes!" Françoise said. "They got the big one at the end. But that's not my favourite. I like the one we bought better, even if it is a bit smaller . . ."

Françoise carried on burbling as we all walked inside together, and now I was in the main room of the gallery, and on the walls around me were the works that had dominated the past year of my life. Sixteen paintings in total. And Nicole was right – they all had a red sticker next to them, indicating that all of them had been sold.

"I added them up," Françoise muttered to me. "You are a millionaire!"

"You see?" A voice behind me said. "I told you you'd become rich and famous in your career."

I spun around. "Oscar!"

I threw my arms around him and hugged him hard. "You came! I didn't think you would."

Oscar smiled. "But I had to come! I wanted to see him."

He cast his gaze around the walls. "I have missed him so much. Until now, I had forgotten how handsome he always was . . ."

Oscar's voice caught a little, choking with emotion as he stared at my paintings. They were of Claude, you see. All sixteen works. Every one of them was a painting of the same black horse with four white socks and a white star on his head. In each of them, my subject was captured in a different pose. In one of the paintings Claude was in motion, cantering free without a rider with his mane and tail flowing in the wind. In another he was caught in close-up so that you could see the details of his muzzle, the whiskers and velvet, the soft sooty blackness of his profile against a bruised lilac sky. And in the big work, the one that the Chapman Gallery had bought, Claude was up on his hind legs rearing and in the background behind his silhouette the streets of Paris were on fire. That one, if the truth were told, was my favourite work too, although I still didn't find it easy to look at even though I had painted it myself. It was called *Terror in Paris*.

A sold-out show, attended by all my friends. For the

next hour I stayed and I tried to enjoy myself, to accept my ascension to the top of the art world. But the truth was, I was not comfortable being the centre of attention, and as soon as I could, I made excuses and slipped away.

I didn't mean to be rude and leave my friends, but I had things to do and someone I needed to see. And so I walked around the loops of the pathway from the Serpentine and into the wooded walkways of Hyde Park itself. There, under a tree, I dug through my bag and I pulled out the book that I always kept with me.

Is it wrong that I never told Nicole Bonifait that I had her great-great-great-grandmother's diary? Yes, I suppose it is. But in all this time, I had found it harder and harder to part with it, to let go of Rose. We were such kindred spirits she and I. So many times I had turned to her pages to try and figure out my own life. It's funny too, to read back over her entries now, knowing what I do, how *Grignons de Camargue* would make her world famous. And yet, even though she had unflinching faith in her talent, she really had no idea what was to come. I opened the diary and I read her final entry . . .

*August 12, 1853*

Aunt Mimi's art critic came today. I knew they were here when I heard the wheels of the carriage outside on the gravel, the horses snorting and the leathers of their harnesses creaking. By the time I had risen from bed, got into my chair and dressed, I could already hear the voices in the drawing room. Familiar voices. I came in to find my aunt laughing and smiling, and on the sofa beside her was none other than Papa and Dorian!

Dorian came running for me and he grasped the handles of my wheelchair and began spinning me around in circles, and I was laughing and dizzy and loving it and begging him to stop at the same time. My brother is such a fool – I do love him.

My greeting to my father was considerably cooler. I still remembered how he had told my aunt that Christmas at Fontainebleau that he couldn't stand the sight of me, that he wanted me gone from Paris. But for his part, he seemed delighted to see me and bent down and kissed my forehead, and when Mimi suggested they must be tired by the journey and perhaps required something to eat and drink, my papa shook his head and said, "First of all, let's do what is important. I want to see what

Rose has been working on. Where is this exciting new painting that you wrote to tell me about?"

And so we all went together, Dorian pushing my wheelchair and Chantal, Mimi and my papa side by side behind us.

"I don't think it is worth all this fuss you are making," I told them as we walked.

"It had better be worth a week-long carriage ride from Paris is all I can say," Dorian teased me.

Had they really come just to see my painting?

When we entered the room and stood in front of it my father said nothing. He stared long and hard and rubbed his beard in mannered consideration. Then he walked back and forth, along the complete length of the work. Finally, he stepped back to the furthest point of the room and looked at the painting in its entirety at a distance, so that he could take it all in at once. And all this time he said nothing! And I sat in my chair and felt my heart pounding in my head and my mouth turn dry with anxiety.

And then, when he did speak at last, his voice had a tremor to it, as if he were about to choke on his own words.

"I should like to be alone with my daughter," he said.

Mimi sighed, and said, "Oh, very well, Jacques, but you don't need to be so dramatic!" And they walked out and left us there.

So I expected the worst now. That my father was disappointed by the work, that he was going to spare me the humiliation of telling me this with everyone watching. Then he spoke, and his words were quite unexpected.

"Mimi tells me that you believe I sent you away because I couldn't stand to look at you crippled in a wheelchair."

I was taken aback. "What?"

"That is what she said to me," my papa said. "Is that true, Rose?"

I began to tremble now. "You tell me," I said. "Is it true?"

My father, reached down, took my hand and clasped it in his own. "No, Rose," he said firmly. "It was because I couldn't stand there and watch helplessly while your very spirit was dying. I didn't want to let you go, but Mimi convinced me that here in the Camargue you would find your strength once more, that your *joie de vivre* – your joy of life would return." He gave a wry smile. "And I see now, looking at this work you have made, that my sister, as usual, was right."

He smiled and looked from me to the painting. "You come from a long line of artists, Rose, but you were always destined to be the greatest of all of us. This painting marks your elevation. With it, you will become the toast of the Paris art world . . ."

So the misunderstanding between Papa and me is over. And now, all I can think is that I should never have held my resentments so hard for so long. For we are a family reunited now for just a brief time. Papa and Dorian plan to return to Paris next week and take *Grignons de Camargue* with them to hand over to Papa's gallerists in the hope they might find a buyer. I will stay behind at Flamants Roses. For this is my home now, and Paris seems a lifetime ago, so perhaps I may never return.

*** 

It is extremely frustrating to me that Rose's diary finishes there on this page. I have turned the pages over and over, hoping that somehow new words will miraculously appear on the blank sheets.

I don't know why the diary ends so abruptly. I like to think that this is because her life became so fabulous after that she didn't have time to write in it any more.

It is one of life's ironies, I think, that we keep diaries just when we are at our most boring, and when things get truly interesting we are too busy. I certainly didn't have time for a diary now! I put Rose's hardbound text back in my bag carefully nestling it there for safekeeping and kept walking.

The light was turning golden and it was that time of day when everything looks prettier than usual. I crossed at the lights heading across Bayswater Road to Hyde Park Mews. These were the stables where the black-and-white cobs that I had once painted to gain entry to the art school lived. It was a pretty cool place to keep a horse. From these stables it was just a quick two-minute ride to reach the bridle paths and arenas of Hyde Park. I remember watching the riders on their horses heading back to the mews after they'd been hacking through the park and thinking they were the luckiest people in the world to have their horses right here in the city. I never thought for one minute that one day I would be one of them, that I'd be able to keep my own horse here too.

"Maisie, hi!" Bonnie the stable girl gave me a wave as I walked through the cobblestoned yard. "I thought it was your exhibition today?"

"It was," I said. "I left early. I wanted to take him out for a ride while the light was still good."

Bonnie laughed. "He'll be pleased. He's missed you today. I mean, you're always here and I think he was in a sulk when I did the feeds today instead. He turned his rump on me."

I laughed. That sounded like my horse all right. He was fiercely loyal. All his life, he'd only had two owners. The first had been the Célestins, and now – now Claude had me.

"Claude?" I opened the stable doors and walked inside and from the far corner of the stall I heard him nicker back to me. There was such a tone to that nicker, though! As if he was accusing me of being late!

"I know, I know, I'm sorry," I told him as I grabbed my brushes and began to groom him. He was literally the most handsome horse in the world, I thought. My muse. My forever horse. With his four white socks and his star, the jet-black coat shining like night. On his hind leg the evidence of his injuries would always be there. After the surgery and the three months he spent on box rest the bone had healed better than anyone could have expected. But the proud flesh that had grown on the wound meant that he never grew the hair on that leg back again, and you could still see quite clearly the scars where the van had struck him. To me, that only made him more handsome – it was a symbol of his courage and his sacrifice.

I used the money from the Lucie's auction and my other sales to buy him from the Célestins and get him here. They had no use for him any more since he could no longer work as a police horse. I worried that Oscar might be upset, but he was delighted when I told him what I'd done. His visit to London was not just to see my show, but to visit the real Claude. At the gallery tonight we'd made plans and tomorrow the two of us were borrowing one of the cobs and were going riding together in Hyde Park.

Yes, riding. They thought Claude was going to die. Then they thought he was too wounded to ever be ridden again. They were wrong. Slowly, carefully, I had nursed him back to health, working a little more each day to strengthen the tendons and muscles in his broken leg. Soon he was walking perfectly soundly, and then trotting and cantering on the lunge. When the vet checked his X-rays and gave me permission to ride him, I cried.

I put my grooming brushes aside and grabbed my

saddle and bridle, tacking up inside the stall before leading Claude out into the cobbled courtyard of the mews and mounting up there. Then I rode him to the Bayswater Road and stood at the lights and waited for the pedestrian signal to bleep so we could cross. Claude's years on the streets of Paris mean that he is the perfect city horse. Even the red double-decker buses here don't make him bat an eyelid. The other day there was a brass band in the park and some protestors with placards, and he just strolled along through it all like a superstar. He makes me feel so safe on his back. And I'm learning to ride. I can rise to the trot, and I can even canter now. You're not supposed to in the park, but at this hour when there are no other riders on the tracks I've been practising.

We reach the bridle path that passes the Serpentine and I think of all those people inside the gallery, the bourgeoisie of London, raising their champagne flutes and talking about art and being fabulous. And I know there is no place I would rather be right now than here with my best friend. And I take up the reins and I close my legs and sit tall and look to the horizon, and I canter on.

EPILOGUE

In New York's Metropolitan Museum of Art on Fifth Avenue, in Gallery 812, you will find one of the most famous paintings of the nineteenth century and the only important painting of this era by a woman – *The Horse Fair* by Rosa Bonheur.

It took Rosa Bonheur almost two years to create her masterpiece, and her commitment to being an artist, despite the extreme sexism towards women painters at the time, marks her out as one of feminism's greatest trailblazers.

Determined to create her art, Bonheur took to dressing as a man to avoid attention when she frequented the abattoirs of Paris, and made her twice weekly visits to the horse markets that took place in the boulevard de l'Hôpital, near the asylum of Salpêtrière. Here, she began to work up her sketches of the horses, the heavy draught Percherons and Boulonnaises and Selle Français, figuring out her plan and mapping out the proportions of her gigantic masterpiece that would end up measuring two and a half metres in height and over five metres in length.

When the work finally went on display in Paris in 1853 nobody believed that a mere woman could possibly have painted such a "masculine" and imposing work of art. In England, critics acclaimed it as the greatest work of its kind and yet there were many who remained adamant that a woman couldn't possibly have created it! To prove them wrong Bonheur was forced to tour alongside her painting so that they could see her in the flesh.

When American art patron Cornelius Vanderbilt II bought the work for a record sum the purchase rocked the art world and secured Rosa Bonheur a place forever as one of the most important artists who ever lived.

The character of Rose Bonifait is based on Rosa Bonheur. As for the rest of this book, well, if you travel to Paris you'll find much of the modern-day story is also based on real life. The Célestins – the stables that are the home of the horses of the Garde républicaine – are right there on the boulevard Henri IV. And Ladurée, the store that is renowned for having the best macarons in the world, has a branch just down the road.

The wild horses of the Camargue are very real too. They are always grey, and it is believed they were once the prized possessions of the Romans, descended from the Arabic Barb. Unlike the Barb, who learnt to survive the hardships of the desert, the Camargue horse has adapted to life in the salt marshes of the French coast-lands. If you visit the Camargue you'll see them cantering wild and free through the waves in the natural wetland reserves that surround the village of Saintes-Maries-de-la-Mer. For centuries they've been tended by the gardians, the French horsemen who manage the herd and muster them twice a year so that they can select young stock ready to be broken into saddle as riding horses, branded with the symbol of their lineage and let loose again to roam wild through the waves on the briny terrain of salt marsh and rice fields.

And if you are in London, visit the Serpentine Gallery, and watch the black-and-white cobs go about their daily exercise in Hyde Park, and then travel across the city to Trafalgar Square to the National Gallery and you'll find a painting by the English artist George Stubbs of a horse called Whistlejacket that was one of the chief inspirations both for Rosa Bonheur and for this story. Whistlejacket's portrait is worth thirteen million pounds, and if I had the money he would be mine.

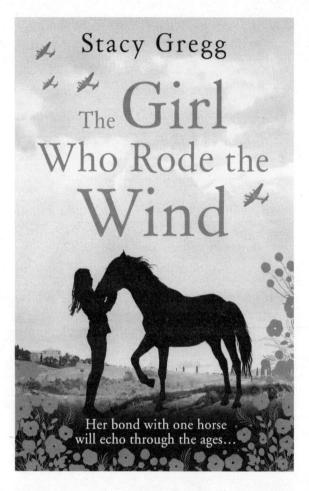

# Stacy Gregg

## The Girl Who Rode the Wind

Her bond with one horse
will echo through the ages…

An epic, emotional story of two girls and their bond
with beloved horses, the action sweeping between Italy
during the Second World War and the present day.

One family's history of adventure and heartbreak –
and how it is tied to the world's most dangerous
horse race, the Palio.